U0080537

哈福

哈福

哈福

哈福

可以馬上學會的

超強英語聽力課

最有效率的聽力訓練法
破解英聽密碼、突破瓶頸

一次搞定：TOEIC・TOEFL・IELTS・英檢・學測・會考

附
MP3

蘇盈盈・卡拉卡 —— 合著

哈福

最有效率的聽力訓練法
破解英聽密碼、突破瓶頸

一次搞定：TOEIC、TOEFL、IELTS、英檢、學測、會考

　　隨著國際化的快速趨勢，為了跟上潮流，學好國際第一通用外語－英語，就是大家眼前最重要的功課。學英語的好處很多：除了可以開拓自己的眼界、結交更多朋友、獲得多元的第一手消息、瀏覽網站更方便等，影響我們最大的，無非是精通英語在職場上佔盡的優勢！想進國際化的大公司，不會英語那就真是 No way 了！

　　學語言，除了希望可以閱讀、欣賞他國文化外，最希望的當然還是能說出流利道地的外文，跟外國人輕鬆溝通囉！為了讓讀者有更親切的學習環境，本公司特別編撰「超強英語」系列，強力增進您的英語能力。書加錄音雙管齊下，讓您彈指翻閱之間，英語實力馬上提升！

　　本書是一本能有效提升聽力實力的優良書籍。本書特別依據聽力訓練法編排，將文章、對話與中譯一併收錄，只要照著每章開頭的說明，循序漸進、重複聆聽，就能跟著書中人物，瓊安、莎拉、布蘭達……一起體驗逐夢樂趣，快速飆高英語實力！本書內容新鮮活潑，除了可以當作訓練英語的最佳教材外，更可立即應用在日常生活中。

本書打破傳統單調的編撰模式，每篇實用會話後，都有字彙補充，加上兩道聽力問題，更貼心地將關鍵字標示出，目的是在訓練您應考時的答題速度。迅速抓出題目與選項的關鍵字，應試時就能從容得高分！

隨著英語教材日漸生活化的趨勢，英語聽力亦應打破傳統制式的學習法，以更符合時代需要的技巧來學習。想要有效提升自我英語實力，聽、說、讀、寫全方位加強，本書絕對是你不可或缺的好幫手。除了實質上提升英聽能力外，更具備了趣味性及實用性，能激發讀者自動自發的學習心，達到事半功倍的成果。

本書由專業英語作家精心撰寫，道地且精彩，讀來趣味橫生。全書 50 單元的流暢會話，帶您進入英語聽力的新境界，跟著作者的精心安排，按部就班學習，英語實力迅速精進。每單元都包括以下四個學習重點：

Start from here 故事背景 每個對話前，都精心歸納出故事背景與說明，訓練讀者聽文章的功力。聽力訓練面面俱到，實力徹底提升！

Dialog 聽力對話 會話內容相當生活化，除了可增進讀者口說表達能力外，更可將文中所學的單字、對話運用到生活上，快速提升您的英語表達實力。

Keywords 聽力關鍵字 從課文精選出來的常用關鍵單字、片語，重複練習，好記好學，讓您一聽到英語就能立即反應，英語聽力拿高分！

Questions 聽力關鍵題 搭配簡潔中譯，與正確答案，讓您快速驗收成果，英語實力更加深厚！

本書內容深入淺出，是一般英語學習者訓練聽力的最佳選擇，也是學生精進英語溝通表達能力的好幫手。

美籍錄音老師實況模擬，專業錄音，搭配學習，效果加倍！

本系列最大特色：

1. 特別設計．聽力測驗： 為呈現原汁原味的美語文章，特聘請英語教材專家撰寫，內容專業、流暢，用字精練，言簡意賅，看完實力馬上突飛猛進！

2. 精彩對白．一次學會： 各種情境的文章、對話，勤加熟讀，英語表達完全無障礙。

3. 嚴謹編撰．專業錄音： 由美籍專業播音員，精心錄製的精質錄音內容，發音純正標準，腔調自然符合情境，讓您跟著道地流暢的語調，快速學會正確美式發音。

4. 聽說能力．同步提升： 精心設計的聽力訓練法，完整紮實的文章、會話、單字、試題，從鴨子聽雷到耳熟能詳，英語聽力技巧即刻掌握！

按部就班跟著本書所設計的學程加以學習，您將迅速進入聽力新境界，英語聽說能力絕對令人眼睛一亮！

編者 謹識

　　本書共有 50 個單元，錄音內容，包括「故事背景」、「聽力對話」、「聽力關鍵字」與「聽力關鍵題」。每單元都標示出錄音軌數，方便讀者按進度訓練時查找。

　　首先，英語老師會按照章節訓練重點，用英語提示讀者學習方法。從基礎熱身到熟稔階段，您可以依自己的情況，事先預習文章、對話，跟著錄音一起讀，或是不看文章，直接聽完內容後作答。錄音內容按照書本順序：

Start from here $\xrightarrow{\text{一遍}}$ Dialog $\xrightarrow{\text{一遍}}$ Keywords $\xrightarrow{\text{二遍}}$
（故事背景）　　（聽力對話）（聽力關鍵字）

Questions $\xrightarrow{\text{作答時間五秒}}$ 完成作答
（聽力關鍵題）

　　按照上列指標循序漸進，是最正確、最有效的學習方式。

　　本 CD 錄音內容，已轉為 MP3 格式，特別邀請專業播音員錄製而成，發音純正，讀者可以聆聽到最道地的美式發音，並習慣外國人的腔調與速度。

　　最後，您可以按照自己的狀況，反覆使用本教材，並將跟不上速度的地方註記起來。隨時給自己的聽力作健診，很快地，您就能突破聽力瓶頸，各項考試都輕鬆過關喔！

CONTENTS

Brenda in the Big City (Part III)
布蘭達在大城市（三）

Chapter 1

Joanne 瓊安

Don't worry that you can't keep up with the CD. In this chapter, you could read each article first, and then read along with the CD.

不要擔心跟不上 CD 的速度，會影響作答。在第一章的部分，你可以先預習每段文章對話，再播放 CD 作聽力測驗。

The Big Decision
重大的決策

Start from here

Joanne was eighteen years old and she had just graduated from high school. She wasn't ready to go to university yet. She hadn't decided what to study and had no idea who she even wanted to be. All she knew was that she had to leave the small town she had spent her whole life in. She had to leave the safety and security of her home to really figure out who she was. She hoped her friends and family would support her in this decision. She knew her mother would be the hardest one to convince that she could make it on her own. She waited until her mother got home from work and then told her she needed to have a talk with her.

中譯

　　瓊安已經十八歲了。高中剛畢業，她還沒準備好當大學生；她不知道要主修什麼，也不清楚自己將來要做什麼。她只知道，她必須離開這個習慣已久的故鄉小鎮。她必須遠離這個穩固、安全的家，去找尋真正的自己。她希望朋友及家人可以支持這個決定，但她也知道要說服媽媽讓她獨立是最難的事。等到媽媽下班回家後，她才跟媽媽說有事要商量。

🎁 Dialog 聽力對話

Mom : What's on your mind, sweetie?

甜心，你有什麼心事？

Joanne : Well, I've been thinking about what I want to do with my life.

嗯，我一直在想自己到底要做什麼。

Mom : You just graduated yesterday!

你昨天才剛畢業呀！

Don't you think you should relax and enjoy the summer?

你難道不認為自己應該要放鬆、享受一下暑期生活？

Joanne : No, I want to get started with my life.

不，我想要開始過真正的生活。

Mom : Well, okay. Why don't you get a job?

那麼，找個工作如何？

Maybe work in a shop?

當個店員呢？

I will give you some pocket money while you're figuring out what you want to do.

你可以邊想未來的路，缺錢時，我再給你零用錢。

I think the flower shop downtown is hiring.

我想市中心的花店應該有缺人。

Joanne : Mom, you don't understand.
媽，你不懂！

I want to move away. I want to do this on my own.
我想要搬出去。我想獨立生活。

Mom : Move? Why do you want to move? Where?
搬出去？為什麼你想搬出去？要搬去哪兒？

Joanne : I want to move to Vancouver.
我想搬去溫哥華住。

Mom : Oh.... that's so far away.
但是那很遠呢。

Joanne : I know Mom, but how else will I know that I can do it?
我知道，媽。但是不這樣，我怎麼知道自己辦不辦得到？

I have to move far away to test myself.
我必須搬到遠方，好考驗自己。

Mom : But you're my only child. I'll be so lonely.
但是我只有你這麼一個孩子。我會很孤單的。

Joanne : I know. I'll miss you so much.
我知道。我一定會很想念你的。

I feel sick about it, but I know this is what I need to do. You have to let me go.
我也不想這樣，可是我一定得這麼做。請你答應讓我離開。

Mom : Well... I suppose you're right.
嗯，我想你說的對。

I love you and though I don't want you to go, I want you to be happy.
我愛你。雖然我不希望你走，但只要你快樂就好。

I'll **support** you with this. Guess we'd better start **packing**!
我支持你。那麼，咱們開始整理行李吧！

Keywords 聽力關鍵字

- ☑ **graduate** — 畢業
- ☑ **safety** — 安全
- ☑ **security** — 安穩
- ☑ **to make it on one's own** — 獨立
- ☑ **sweetie** — 甜心
- ☑ **figure something out** — 思考出……
- ☑ **support** — 支持
- ☑ **decision** — 決策
- ☑ **pocket money** — 零用錢
- ☑ **pack** — 打包

Questions 聽力關鍵題

1. _____

Ⓐ She wanted to go to university.
Ⓑ She wanted to **figure out** who she was.
Ⓒ She wanted to find new friends.
Ⓓ She didn't want to live with her mother anymore.

2. _____

Ⓐ She wanted to convince her mother that she could **make it on her own**.
Ⓑ She wanted money for her trip.
Ⓒ She needed help to decide what to do with her life.
Ⓓ She was bored because she didn't have to go to school anymore.

Answers and Translations 聽力中譯與解答

1. Why did Joanne want to leave the **safety** and **security** of her home?
為什麼瓊安想離開這個穩固、安全的家？

Ⓐ 她想要上大學。　　Ⓑ 她想要思考自己未來的人生。
Ⓒ 她想要交新朋友。　Ⓓ 她不想再和媽媽同住。

2. Why did Joanne want to have a talk with her mother?
為什麼瓊安想和媽媽談一談？

Ⓐ 她想要說服媽媽讓自己獨立。　Ⓑ 她想要旅費。
Ⓒ 她要媽媽幫她決定未來的人生。　Ⓓ 因為畢業了，她覺得很無聊。

答案：1→B　2→A

Unit 2

The First Night Away From Home

離家第一夜

Track-3

Start from here

As the pilot announced the plane was preparing to land, Joanne looked out the window to see the city she would be calling home. Even in the dark she could see how tall the buildings were. The city was so big and bright, and it seemed to go on forever. It was at least ten times bigger than her hometown. She was amazed at how many cars were on the freeways. She was overwhelmed with a feeling of nausea. Joanne felt scared about being alone in this big, new place.

After the plane landed and she got her luggage, Joanne hailed a taxi. The taxi took her to a hostel downtown. It was too late to walk around the neighborhood and she was tired, so she got into bed and tried to sleep. The girl in the bunk bed above her leaned over to talk to her.

中譯

　　當駕駛員宣布飛機即將著陸時，瓊安注視窗外，看著這個她準備落腳的新城市。在黑暗中，她仍可看出相當高聳的大廈。這城市又大又亮麗，似乎永無止境的延伸。跟家鄉比起來，這裡至少大了十倍。高速公路上多得數不清的車輛，讓瓊安感到驚奇。她陷入暈眩之中。獨自置身在這大而陌生的新地方，讓她心生畏懼。

　　飛機降落後，她取得行李，並招了一輛計程車。計程車載她到市區的宿舍。天色已晚不好四處走，加上她也累了，所以她打算就寢。上舖的女孩側身和她聊天。

🎁 Dialog 聽力對話

Lila : Hi! I'm Lila. What's your name?
嗨！我是麗拉。你叫什麼名字？

Joanne : Joanne. Where are you from?
我是瓊安。你是哪裡人？

Lila : I'm from Germany. I'm here doing some traveling for the summer. What about you?
我是德國人。我利用暑假來這裡旅遊。你呢？

Joanne : I moved here today. This is my first night in Vancouver.
我今天剛搬來這兒。這是我在溫哥華的第一晚。

Lila : Really? Wow, you're going to have a great time. I've been here for three weeks and I love it here. The people are friendly, the weather is fantastic and the beaches are amazing.

真的嗎？哇！你一定會玩得很開心的。我已經到這兒三個星期了，我很愛這裡。居民很友善，氣候宜人，海灘也很棒。

Joanne : Were you scared when you first got here?

你剛到這裡的時候，會不會害怕？

Lila : Of course! That's normal. It's a whole new **environment** and it takes a little while to feel comfortable. Look at it like an adventure!

當然！這是人之常情。到一個全新的環境，總需要一點時間來適應，就把它當作冒險囉。

Joanne : I'm nervous I won't meet anyone or anything. Maybe I've made a mistake.

我擔心我交不到朋友，遇不到新鮮事。或許來這兒是個錯誤。

Lila : Don't worry. All those things will come in time. Why don't you **hang out with** me tomorrow?

別擔心。這些以後都會有的。明天何不和我一起去走走？

I'll show you around and help you **get acquainted with** the city.

我可以帶你四處逛逛，幫你熟悉這座城市。

Joanne : Really? That would be great! Thanks so much.
真的？那真的太好了！謝謝。

Lila : See? I told you things would work out. You've only been here an hour and you've already made a friend : me!
你看？我就説沒問題的嘛！你才剛到一個小時而已，就交上我這個朋友了！

Keywords 聽力關鍵字

☑ **pilot** 駕駛員

☑ **overwhelmed** 感到震撼

☑ **nausea** 反胃；暈眩

☑ **luggage** 行李

☑ **hail a taxi** 招計程車

☑ **bunk bed** 臥床；睡舖

☑ **lean over** 俯身傾向

☑ **environment** 環境

☑ **hang out with someone** 與……在一起

☑ **get acquainted with something / someone** 熟悉

Questions 聽力關鍵題

1. _____

Ⓐ She always gets airsick in airplanes.
Ⓑ She is afraid of heights.
Ⓒ She felt scared and worried about being alone in such a big place.
Ⓓ The plane food was making her sick.

2. _____

Ⓐ She was afraid to go out at night.
Ⓑ The hostel rules wouldn't allow it.
Ⓒ She was still feeling sick.
Ⓓ She was tired after such a long flight.

Answers and Translations 聽力中譯與解答

1. Why was Joanne overcome with a feeling of nausea?
為什麼瓊安覺得暈眩、不舒服？

Ⓐ 因為她一直都；會暈機。　　Ⓑ 因為她有懼高症。
Ⓒ 因為她擔心及害怕獨自待在這個大城市裡。
Ⓓ 飛機上的食物讓她作嘔。

2. Why didn't Joanne walk around and look at the city after she arrived at the hostel?
為什麼瓊安在抵達宿舍後，不到處走一走，瀏覽一下這座城市？

Ⓐ 她不敢晚上外出。　　　　Ⓑ 宿舍規定不准外出。
Ⓒ 她仍然不舒服。　　　　　Ⓓ 長途飛行後，她已經很疲倦了。

答案：1→C　2→D

Joanne Gets an Apartment

瓊安找到公寓

Track-4

Start from here

Joanne sipped her coffee as she read through the apartment rental listings in the newspaper. She had been staying at the hostel for a few days now and she was ready to have her own space. The only problem was Vancouver was an expensive place to live in and she didn't have very much money. Her family was helping her out a bit with money but it still didn't add up to much. She wanted to live alone but after looking at a few apartments in the price range she could afford, she realized it wasn't an option. She needed a roommate. She scanned the Roommates Wanted section of the newspaper. One ad caught her attention. It read: *New to the city? Come live with me! I'm looking for a responsible woman who is fun, outgoing, and easy to talk to. I live in a two-bedroom condo near the beach and want a great person to live with. $300 / month. Call Julie. Tel: 2345-8790.* Joanne was so excited. It sounded perfect and was right in her price range. She called Julie right away and set up a meeting for that afternoon.

As Joanne climbed the steps of the condo where Julie lived, she was filled with excitement.

中譯

　　瓊安邊讀著報紙的公寓出租廣告，邊啜飲著咖啡。她已經住了幾天宿舍，現在她已經準備好要找一個屬於自己的地方。唯一的問題是，溫哥華的生活花費高，而她的錢不多。雖然家人會支助她，但總共加起來，幫助還是不大。本來她想自己住，但看過一些預算範圍內的房子後，她發現這行不通；她得要找個室友才行。她看了報紙的徵室友欄廣告，其中一則吸引她的眼光：剛到這城市嗎？來和我住吧！我正在找一位負責、風趣、外向、談得來的女室友。本公寓有兩間臥室，近海邊，希望尋得一好室友。租金每月三百元。請電洽茱莉；電話：2345-8790。瓊安很興奮，這簡直太完美了，租金也合乎預算。於是，她馬上打電話給茱莉，約好當天下午見面。

　　瓊安步上茱莉公寓的階梯，她滿心雀躍。

🎁 Dialog 聽力對話

Julie　: Hi! You must be Joanne! Come on in!
　　　　嗨！你一定是瓊安吧！請進。

Joanne : Thanks. Wow! This place is beautiful!
　　　　謝謝。哇！這地方很漂亮。

Julie	:	Yeah, I love it. It's so bright and sunny and it's close to everything. So, tell me about yourself.

嗯，我很愛這裡。光線明亮，陽光充足，到哪裡都很近。那麼，談談你自己吧。

Joanne	:	Well, I'm really new to the city. I'm from a small town in **the Prairies**. This is the first time I've ever been anywhere without my family but I wanted to take a chance and try to figure out what I want to do and who I am.

呃，我第一次來這個城市。家鄉在大草原區的一座小鎮，這是我第一次不靠家人，獨立生活。不過，我想藉此機會找出自己的人生方向。

Julie	:	That's really brave of you.

你真的很勇敢。

Joanne	:	Brave?

勇敢？

Julie	:	Yeah, it takes a lot of **courage** to walk away from all you know. You must have the heart of a **warrior**.

是啊！離開自己所熟悉的一切，需要很大的勇氣。你一定有勇士精神。

Joanne	:	Oh, I don't feel very brave. I feel very afraid.

噢，我不覺得勇敢，我反倒很害怕。

Julie	:	I have a good feeling about you, Joanne. Would you like to be my new roommate?

我滿欣賞你的，瓊安，你願意當我的新室友嗎？

Joanne ： I'd love to!
　　　　 我很樂意！

Keywords 聽力關鍵字

☑ **rental listings** 　　　　　　　　　　 出租表
☑ **afford** 　　　　　　　　　　 負擔得起
☑ **scan** 　　　　　　　　　　 過濾；掃描
☑ **outgoing** 　　　　　　　　　　 外向的
☑ **condominium (condo)** 　　　　　　　　　　 公寓
☑ **right away** 　　　　　　　　　　 馬上
☑ **the Prairies** 　　　　　　　　　　 大草原
☑ **warrior** 　　　　　　　　　　 戰士
☑ **courage** 　　　　　　　　　　 勇氣
☑ **price range** 　　　　　　　　　　 價位

MEMO

....

....

....

....

....

....

Questions 聽力關鍵題

1. _____

Ⓐ She was afraid to live on her own.
Ⓑ She couldn't afford to live by herself.
Ⓒ She needed a servant.
Ⓓ She needed a mother.

2. _____

Ⓐ Julie thought living alone needed a lot of courage.
Ⓑ Julie thought it took a warrior to live alone.
Ⓒ She wanted to live with a warrior.
Ⓓ A warrior told her so.

Answers and Translations 聽力中譯與解答

1. Why did Joanne need to find a roommate?
   為什麼瓊安需要找一位室友？

   Ⓐ 她害怕自己一個人住。　　Ⓑ 她負擔不起獨自生活的費用。
   Ⓒ 她需要一位傭人。　　　　Ⓓ 她需要一位媽媽。

2. Why did Julie said "you must have the heart of a warrior"?
   為什麼茱莉說「你要有勇士的決心」？

   Ⓐ 茱莉認為搬出來自己住要有很大的勇氣。
   Ⓑ 茱莉認為只有勇士才能獨居。
   Ⓒ 她想跟勇士一起住。
   Ⓓ 勇士跟她說的。

答案：1→B 2→A

Unit 4

Joanne Calls Home

瓊安打電話回家

Start from here

As Joanne settled into bed in her new apartment, she smiled. She had made it through her first week in Vancouver. Julie was right: she was brave. For the first time since she left home she felt like things were going to be okay. She thought she had made the right decision. She decided to call her Mom to tell her how great things were going so she wouldn't worry. She quickly dialed the number.

中譯

　　瓊安窩在新公寓的床上，臉上露出了笑容。她已經過了在溫哥華的第一個禮拜。茉莉說得沒錯：她很勇敢。自從離家後，她第一次覺得未來的日子將會很順利，她認為自己的決定是正確的。她決定打電話給媽媽，告訴她事情進展得很順利，並請她不要擔心。她很快速地撥了號碼。

🎁 Dialog 聽力對話

Mom : Hello?
　　　哈囉？

| Joanne | : | Hi Mom, it's me.
嗨，媽，是我。 |

| Mom | : | Hi honey! How are you doing? I miss you so much!
嗨，親愛的！你好嗎？我好想你！ |

| Joanne | : | I miss you, too. Things are going so well, Mom. I already have one friend and today I found an apartment and a roommate! My friend's name is Lila. She's from Germany. My roommate's name is Julie, and she says I have the heart of a warrior!
我也很想你。媽媽，一切都很順利。我已經交了一個朋友；今天我找到公寓和新室友了。我的朋友叫麗拉，她是德國人；而室友叫茱莉，她說我有勇士精神。 |

| Mom | : | That's great.
那很好。 |

| Joanne | : | You don't sound very excited.
你好像不是很高興的樣子。 |

| Mom | : | No, I am. I guess I was just hoping you would hate it so much you would want to come home. I miss your face.
不，我很高興。大概是因為我以為你不喜歡那裡，要回來了。我真的很想你。 |

| Joanne | : | Oh, Mom, I need you to be happy for me.
噢，媽，我希望你為我感到高興。 |

Mom : I know. It's just so lonely here without you. I don't have anyone to talk to anymore.

我知道。只是這裡少了你，真是太孤單了。再也沒有人和我聊天了。

Joanne : Mom, you should see this as an opportunity to make new friends.

媽，你應該把這當成交新朋友的好機會啊！

Mom : I'm too old to make friends, Joanne.

我已經太老，交不到朋友了，瓊安。

Joanne : Mom! You're never too old to make friends. Join a club or do some charity work. That way you'll meet people with the same interests as you. If you meet someone you like, just ask him or her out for lunch or something.

媽，交朋友永遠不嫌遲。你可以加入俱樂部或慈善活動，這麼一來，你可以結交到志同道合的朋友。如果你交了喜歡的朋友，就可以邀他們一起吃飯或什麼的。

Mom : Listen to you, my shy little daughter giving me advice on meeting people.

你聽聽，我害羞的小女兒竟然要教我怎麼交朋友了！

Joanne : I've learned a lot about myself in the last week.

這個禮拜以來，我已經對自己更了解了。

Mom : Yes, you even sound different. I don't know...

是啊！你連聲音聽起來都不同了！我不知道……

29

Joanne : Really? How?
真的嗎？哪裡不同？

Mom : You just sound more grown up.
只是聽起來更懂事了吧。

Joanne : So, will you try to make some new friends?
那麼，你會去交一些新朋友嗎？

Mom : I'll try. I love you, Joanne.
我會試試看。我愛你，瓊安。

Joanne : I love you too, Mom. Goodnight.
我也愛你，媽媽。晚安。

Mom : Goodnight, my love.
晚安，親愛的。

Keywords 聽力關鍵字

☑ **settle**	穩定
☑ **dial**	撥（電話）
☑ **opportunity**	機會
☑ **join**	加入
☑ **club**	俱樂部
☑ **charity work**	慈善公益
☑ **interest**	興趣

1. _____

Ⓐ She got some bad news at work.
Ⓑ She made some bad friends.
Ⓒ She misses her daughter and she is lonely.
Ⓓ She thinks Joanne is growing up.

2. _____

Ⓐ She hates **charity work**.
Ⓑ She doesn't like **clubs**.
Ⓒ She can't ask people out for lunch.
Ⓓ She is too old to make new friends.

Answers and Translations 聽力中譯與解答

1. Why does Joanne's mother sound sad on the phone?
   1. 為什麼瓊安的媽媽在電話上，聲音聽起來很難過？

   Ⓐ 她在工作上得知壞消息。　　**Ⓑ** 她交到了壞朋友。
   Ⓒ 她想念她的女兒，而且她很孤單。　**Ⓓ** 她認為瓊安正在長大。

2. Why does Joanne's mother think she can't make new friends?
   2. 為什麼瓊安的媽媽認為自己不能交新朋友？

   Ⓐ 她討厭公益活動。　　**Ⓑ** 她不喜歡俱樂部。
   Ⓒ 她不能邀請朋友外出共進午餐。　**Ⓓ** 她已經不是交新朋友的年紀了。

答案：1→C　2→D

Joanne Gets a Job

瓊安找到工作

Track-6

Start from here

As the days and weeks passed, Joanne spent a great deal of time and money exploring her new city. She went sightseeing, she went whale watching and she did some shopping. She was quickly running out of money. Joanne had to get a job if she was going to survive in Vancouver. She scanned the Want Ads in the newspaper looking for a job that sounded like fun, or at least one that she could do. She didn't find anything. One day, when she was out for a walk in her neighborhood, she passed a Doggy Daycare. She had never seen one before. People who didn't want to leave their pets alone all day could take them there so that they could play with other dogs. She stepped inside to check it out. A man sat behind the front counter.

中譯

隨著時間的過去，瓊安花了許多時間與金錢探索新城市。她到處觀光、賞鯨、及逛街購物，很快她就把錢花光了。如果她打算在溫哥華待下去，她就得找工作。她看了報紙的求

職版，想要找個看起來有趣，或至少她可以做的工作。但是，
卻什麼也沒找到。有一天，她在家附近散步，經過了一間狗
店。之前，她從未看過這樣的商店：當主人不想放寵物單獨
在家時，可以把狗兒送來，讓牠們有其他的狗伴。她走進去
一探究竟，一位男士坐在櫃檯的後方。

 Dialog 聽力對話

Russ : Hi! What can I do for you?
嗨！我能為您效勞嗎？

Joanne : Oh, I just wanted to have a look. I've never seen
a place like this before and I really love dogs.
呃，我只是看看而已。我從沒看過這種店，再說我也很喜
歡狗。

Russ : Really? Would you like to come out the back and
meet some of the dogs?
真的嗎？你要不要到後面來看其他的狗？

Joanne : Are you sure? I don't want to **impose**.
真的可以？我不想讓你為難。

Russ : No, not at all. Come on back.
一點也不會。來吧。

(Russ takes Joanne out the back to meet the dogs.)
（洛斯帶瓊安到後面看狗。）

Joanne : Oh! There are so many! They're **licking** my hands!

好多狗！牠們在舔我的手耶！

Russ : Wow, I've never seen them like someone so much. Normally they're very afraid of new people.

哇！我從沒見過牠們這麼喜歡一個人！平常，牠們都很怕生的。

Joanne : They must know that I just want to say hello.

牠們一定知道我只是想打聲招呼而已。

Russ : You seem really comfortable with them.

你似乎一點都不怕狗呢。

Joanne : Oh, I had plenty of dogs when I was growing up. Sometimes I feel like I truly understand them.

嗯，我成長的過程中養過很多狗。有時候，我覺得我真的了解牠們。

Russ : I don't normally do this, but would you like to work here?

我平常不會這樣，不過你願意來這裡工作嗎？

Joanne : Are you kidding? Of course I'd love to work here. Why do you ask?

你在開玩笑嗎？我當然希望在這裡工作。你為什麼這麼問？

Russ　：Well, my last **employee** just quit yesterday and I need someone right away. Can you start tomorrow?

這個嘛，上個員工昨天剛離職，我馬上需要人遞補。你可以明天就開始上班嗎？

Joanne　：Yes! That would be so great! I can't believe it. I have a job!

可以！那就太棒了！真不敢相信，我有工作了！

Russ　：I think this is going to work out. See you tomorrow?

我想一定沒問題的。明天見？

Joanne　：**You bet**.

沒問題。

Keywords 聽力關鍵字

☑ **explore**　　　　　　　　　　　　　探索

☑ **sightsee**　　　　　　　　　　　　　觀光

☑ **to check something out**　　　　　查看一下

☑ **counter**　　　　　　　　　　　　　櫃檯

☑ **whale**　　　　　　　　　　　　　　鯨魚

☑ **impose**　　　　　　　　　　　　　強迫

☑ **lick**　　　　　　　　　　　　　　　舔

☑ **employee**　　　　　　　　　　　　員工

☑ **you bet**　　　　　　　　　　　　　沒問題

Questions 聽力關鍵題

1. _____

- Ⓐ She found whale watching job.
- Ⓑ She found a sight-seeing job.
- Ⓒ She found a doggy daycare job.
- Ⓓ She didn't find anything.

2. _____

- Ⓐ Because they lick her hands.
- Ⓑ Because the dogs are afraid of her.
- Ⓒ She had plenty of dogs when she was growing up.
- Ⓓ She thinks dogs are cute and cuddly.

Answers and Translations 聽力中譯與解答

1. What kind of job did Joanne find in the newspaper?
   1. 瓊安在報紙中找到什麼工作？

   Ⓐ 她找到賞鯨的工作。　　Ⓑ 她找到觀光的工作。
   Ⓒ 她找到看養小狗的工作。　Ⓓ 她什麼也沒找到。

2. Why is Joanne comfortable with the dogs?
   2. 為什麼瓊安可以和小狗相處得很好？

   Ⓐ 因為牠們舔她的手。　　Ⓑ 因為狗怕她。
   Ⓒ 因為很多狗陪她一起長大。　Ⓓ 因為她認為狗很可愛。

答案：1→D　2→C

Unit 6

Joanne's First Day at Work

瓊安工作的第一天

 Track-7

Start from here

After a sleepless night, the day finally arrived: Joanne's first big day at work at Happy Tails Doggy Daycare. She was so excited. Her boss, Russ, greeted her warmly and showed her the ropes. She learned how to deal with the dogs when they were misbehaving and how to make sure all the dogs got along and had a fun time at daycare. She was doing so well, Russ decided that he could trust her to work alone while he went out for lunch with a friend from out of town. He smiled at her as he left. Joanne was very nervous but confident she could handle the responsibility.

Suddenly, a man walked in: Joanne's first customer! He was looking for a gift for his new puppy. Joanne showed him some puppy toys.

中譯

　　失眠整晚，天終於亮了：瓊安的「快樂尾巴狗狗寵物店」工作即將展開。她覺得很刺激！老闆洛斯親切地跟她打招呼，並教她工作上的訣竅。她學到了當狗兒不乖的時候，該如何處理？如何讓每一隻狗和樂相處？因為她表現得很好，在洛斯要出去跟遠來的朋友吃飯時，他可以放心地讓瓊安單獨顧店。他離開時，還對瓊安微笑。瓊安雖然很緊張，卻有信心可以扛起責任。

　　突然，一位男士走進來。這是瓊安的第一個客人！男士想幫自己的新小狗買個禮物，瓊安介紹一些狗的玩具給他。

🎁 Dialog 聽力對話

Joanne : What about this rope toy? Puppies love to **chew**!
這個玩具繩圈怎麼樣呢？小狗都很喜歡咬東西！

Man : That looks perfect! I'll take it!
看起來很棒！我買了！

Joanne : The total cost is $14.95.
總共是十四塊九五。

Man : Oh no! I don't have my **wallet**. My **wallet** is in my coat and so are my keys and the problem is that I just **locked** my coat in the **trunk** of my car!
糟了！我沒帶錢包。我的皮夾和鑰匙都在外套裡，可是我的外套卻被鎖在後車廂！

Joanne : Uh oh. What can I do to help?

呃，我能幫上什麼忙嗎？

Man : I'll call the **towing company** and they can get my keys out. May I borrow your phone?

我要打電話給拖吊公司，他們可以幫我取出鑰匙。我可以借個電話嗎？

Joanne : Sure! It's just over there.

當然可以！就在那裡。

Man : (on the phone) Hi, I've **locked** my keys in my car and I need you to get them out for me. Will you come? Okay?

（電話中）嗨！我把鑰匙鎖在車子裡了！請你們來幫我好嗎？可以嗎？

Joanne : Are they coming?

他們會來嗎？

Man : Yes. I have to meet them up the street but they want $40 to do it. Can I borrow $40 from you and I'll pay you back when I get my **wallet**?

會，我要到街上和他們碰面，可是他們要收四十元處理費。我可以向你借四十元嗎？等我拿回皮夾後，我就還你。

Joanne : Oh, I'm not sure. This is my first day. I don't want to get in **trouble**.

我不知道這樣好不好，今天是我第一天上班。我不想惹麻煩。

Man : Don't worry. I'll pay you **right back**.
用不著擔心。我會還你的。

Joanne : Okay, I'll take some money out of the **cash register**. Here you go.
好吧！我從收銀機中拿一些錢出來。拿去吧！

Man : Thanks! I'll be right back. I really owe you one!
謝啦！我馬上回來！我真的欠你一個人情！

Joanne : I hope he gets back before my boss does.
我希望他在老闆回來前就出現。

Keywords 聽力關鍵字

☑	greet	迎接
☑	show someone the ropes	指引某人
☑	chew	咬、嚼
☑	customer	客戶
☑	wallet	皮夾
☑	lock	鎖
☑	trunk	後行李廂
☑	towing company	拖吊公司
☑	trouble	麻煩
☑	be right back	馬上回來
☑	cash register	收銀機

Questions 聽力關鍵題

1. _____

Ⓐ Because she loved dogs.
Ⓑ Because she was misbehaving.
Ⓒ Because he was hungry.
Ⓓ Because she was doing so well.

2. _____

Ⓐ Because she missed the boss.
Ⓑ Because she was lazy.
Ⓒ Because her boss was strange.
Ⓓ Because she didn't want any **trouble** for the first day.

Answers and Translations 聽力中譯與解答

1. Why did the boss think he could leave Joanne alone on her first day?
   為什麼老闆放心讓瓊安第一天上班就單獨顧店？

   Ⓐ 因為她愛狗。　　　　　Ⓑ 因為她表現不好。
   Ⓒ 因為她很餓。　　　　　Ⓓ 因為她表現得很好。

2. Why did Joanne hope that the man could get back before her boss did?
   為什麼瓊安希望陌生人在老闆回來前出現？

   Ⓐ 因為她想念老闆。　　　Ⓑ 因為她懶惰。
   Ⓒ 因為她老闆是個怪人。　Ⓓ 因為她不希望上班第一天就出狀況。

答案：1→D　2→D

41

Joanne Learns a Hard Lesson

瓊安得到的教訓

 Track-8

Start from here

Joanne played with the dogs at the Doggy Daycare while her boss, Russ, was at lunch. She waited for the man she had lent the money to return. She looked out the window, but didn't see any sign of him. An hour passed and Russ returned from lunch. Joanne's heart began to beat quickly. She was worried Russ would be angry if he found out she had taken the money from the cash register. Russ noticed Joanne was acting a little anxious and asked if anything was wrong.

中譯

　　洛斯外出吃午餐的時候，瓊安在寵物店和狗兒一起玩，並等著跟她借錢的那個人回來。她注視著窗外，但是絲毫不見那個人的蹤影。一個鐘頭過去，洛斯吃完午餐回來了！瓊安的心跳開始加速，她擔心當洛斯發現她從收銀機拿了錢後會很生氣。洛斯發現瓊安的神情有些焦慮，於是詢問她出了什麼事。

🎁 Dialog 聽力對話

Russ : Are you okay, Joanne? You seem upset.
瓊安，你還好吧？你看起來不開心。

Joanne : No. I'm fine.
沒有，我很好。

Russ : Are you sure?
真的？

Joanne : Okay, while you were gone, a **man** came in to buy something but he said he'd locked his keys and his wallet in his car. He said he needed money to pay the towing company to unlock it.
好啦，你走了以後，有個男的進來買東西。他說他的鑰匙和皮夾都鎖在車子裡，還說他要借錢請拖吊公司來開鎖。

I gave him money from the cash register.
所以我就從收銀機裡拿了錢借他。

He said he would be right back but that was more than an hour ago.
他說他馬上就會回來，但是都已經過了一個多小時了！

Russ : Joanne, you've been conned.
瓊安，你被騙了！

Joanne : What do you mean?
什麼意思？

Russ : That man was lying about everything. He just wanted the money.
那個人説的全是一派胡言，他只想騙錢。

Joanne : You mean he didn't want to buy anything at all?
你是説他根本不想買東西？

Russ : No.
沒錯。

Joanne : That's so mean! How could he do that?
好過份！他怎麼能這樣？

Russ : I don't know. I guess he doesn't care who he hurts, as long as he gets his money.
我也不知道。我想他只要錢，根本不在乎傷害別人。

Joanne : I'm so sorry, Russ. I'll pay you back as soon as I can.. Oh, I feel so stupid.
對不起，洛斯。我一有錢，就馬上還你。喔，我覺得自己好蠢。

Russ : Don't worry. I'm not going to fire you.
放心，我不會辭掉你的。

Joanne : You're not? Oh, thank goodness.
你不會嗎？謝天謝地。

Russ : Just remember what you learned today. You can't trust everybody.

千萬記得今天得到的教訓：不是所有人都值得信任。

Joanne : No, I guess I can't. Next time I won't be so naive.

不會了！下次我不會這麼天真了。

Keywords 聽力關鍵字

- ☑ **a sign of someone / something**　　　有……徵兆
- ☑ **con**　　　騙錢
- ☑ **pay somebody back**　　　還給…人
- ☑ **naive**　　　天真
- ☑ **fire someone**　　　解雇

MEMO

....

....

....

....

....

....

....

Questions 聽力關鍵題

1. _____

Ⓐ He knew someone had taken the money.
Ⓑ He counted the money and knew some was missing.
Ⓒ The dogs looked unhappy.
Ⓓ Joanne seemed anxious and worried.

2. _____

Ⓐ Puppy toys.
Ⓑ Money.
Ⓒ To use the phone.
Ⓓ A tow truck.

Answers and Translations 聽力中譯與解答

1. Why did the boss ask Joanne if anything was wrong?
   為什麼老闆詢問瓊安出了什麼問題？

   Ⓐ 他知道有人拿了錢。　　Ⓑ 他數了錢，知道丟了一些錢。
   Ⓒ 狗兒們看起來不高興。　　Ⓓ 瓊安看起來焦慮、不安。

2. What did the man shopping for puppy toys really want from the store?
   那位說要買寵物玩具的男子其實想要什麼？

   Ⓐ 小狗玩具。　　Ⓑ 錢。
   Ⓒ 使用電話。　　Ⓓ 拖吊車。

答案：1→D　2→B

The Test

考驗

Start from here

As Joanne walked home from work, she became more and more upset about the man who had lied to her. Nothing like this had ever happened to her before and she couldn't stop thinking about it. She began to doubt her decision to live in a big city. Something like this would never have happened in the small town where she used to live. Maybe the big city wasn't the place for her after all. As she unlocked the door to her apartment she bumped into Julie who was rushing out.

中譯

　　瓊安下班走路回家，越想到那個騙她錢的人就越難過。因為以前不曾發生過這種事，所以瓊安無法不去想它。她也開始懷疑，到大城市的決定是不是錯了。像今天這樣的事，絕不可能發生在她的故鄉小鎮。也許大城市根本不適合她。當她打開公寓門時，正巧遇到跑出門的茉莉。

🎁 Dialog 聽力對話

Julie : Hi, Joanne! I'm just on my way out for a run. Do you want to come?

嗨！瓊安！我正要出去跑步。你要一起來嗎？

Joanne : Um, no thanks. I don't feel like doing anything right now.

呃，不，謝啦！我現在什麼都不想做。

Julie : Are you okay? You seem sad or something.

你還好吧？你看起來有點難過。

Joanne : I'm just starting to wonder if I did the right thing moving here. I left my mother all alone. Perhaps I should have waited until I was older to move away. It's not fair to leave her all alone.

我只是開始懷疑，我到這裡來是不是錯了。我離開媽媽，讓她孤單一人。也許我應該再等長大一點才搬走，留她一個人在那很不公平。

Julie : Where is this coming from?

你怎麼突然這麼想？

Joanne : Don't worry about me. You should go on your run.

別擔心我，你去跑步吧。

Julie : That can wait. You want to get a coffee and talk about this?

這不急。要不要喝杯咖啡，一起聊聊？

Joanne : Okay.

好。

Joanne told Julie all about her awful day at work over a cup of coffee and a piece of cheesecake. When she was finished, Julie sighed.

在咖啡、起司蛋糕的陪伴下，瓊安把上班遇到的不愉快全說給茉莉聽。茉莉聽完後，嘆了一口氣。

Julie : Well, you have two ways of dealing with this. The first one you already know. You can see it as a **sign** that this was a mistake and **head back** home to take care of your mother.

你可以用兩種眼光來看待這件事。第一，你已經知道了；你可以把它看成一種錯誤的訊息，回家照顧你媽。

Joanne : Yes, I think you're right.

嗯，我想你說的對。

Julie : Or, you can see it as a test.

或者，你可以把它當成一種考驗。

Joanne : A test?

一種考驗？

Julie : Remember when I said you have the heart of a **warrior**?

還記得我說過你有勇士的精神嗎？

Joanne : Yes.

記得。

Julie : A warrior must be tested to see if she is strong enough for battle. This is a test, Joanne. How you choose to deal with it will decide if you are ready for battle. How brave are you?

勇士必須通過考驗，證明自己能夠面臨挑戰。瓊安，這是一個考驗。你如何面對，決定了你是否準備好要上陣。你夠勇敢嗎？

Joanne : I don't know.

我不知道。

Julie : You must look in your heart for the answer.

你必須詢問自己內心，找出答案。

Keywords 聽力關鍵字

☑ doubt	懷疑
☑ bump into	撞上
☑ rush	衝跑；急忙行事
☑ fair	公平的
☑ head back	回頭
☑ deal with something / someone	處理
☑ sign	徵兆
☑ warrior	勇士
☑ battle	戰爭

Questions 聽力關鍵題

1. _____

Ⓐ Nothing like that had ever happened to her before.
Ⓑ She missed her small town.
Ⓒ She was starting to hate the big city.
Ⓓ She had too much time on her walk home from work.

2. _____

Ⓐ In the book.
Ⓑ In her heart.
Ⓒ In her house.
Ⓓ In her cheesecake.

Answers and Translations 聽力中譯與解答

1. Why couldn't Joanne stop thinking about the man who stole the money from her?
   為什麼瓊安一直想著騙她錢的那位男子？

   Ⓐ 這種事以前不曾發生在她身上。　Ⓑ 她想念家鄉的小鎮。
   Ⓒ 她開始憎惡大城市。　Ⓓ 下班回家的路上，她的時間太多了。

2. Where does Julie tell Joanne to look for the answer?
   茱莉要瓊安到哪裡找答案？

   Ⓐ 書中。　Ⓑ 心裡。
   Ⓒ 房子裡。　Ⓓ 起司蛋糕裡。

答案：1→A　2→B

Unit 9

The Battlefield

戰場

🔘 Track-10

Start from here

     As Joanne brushed her teeth that night, she thought about what Julie had said to her in the coffee shop. She was so confused. She missed her home so much and this new adventure of hers wasn't turning out the way she thought. She climbed into bed and switched off the light. She stared up at the ceiling, hoping the answer to her question would come soon. Before she knew it, she fell asleep. Suddenly, she found herself in a large clearing. She looked around in shock. She could hear people screaming in the distance and the thunderous sound of horses' hooves. She turned around to find herself in the middle of a battlefield. She looked down and discovered she was wearing a suit of armor and clasped in her hand was a sword. She heard a voice behind her. It was her leader.

中譯

     當晚瓊安一邊刷牙，一邊想起茱莉在咖啡店對她說的話。她真的很困惑。她很想家，而且這個冒險之旅跟她當初預期的不一樣。她上了床，關上燈；注視著天花板，希望馬上找出心中的答案。不知不覺，她睡著了。突然！她發現自己置身於一片廣大的空地。她震驚地看著四周：她聽得到遠處有人在尖叫吶喊，以及轟隆隆的馬蹄聲。她轉身發現自己置身於戰場上，往下一望，更發現自己身著盔甲，手中緊握著一把劍。她聽到背後出現一個聲音：那是她的領袖所發出的。

 ## Dialog 聽力對話

Leader : Things look **bleak**, little one. Most of our men have died and the **enemy** seems to be growing in strength.

士兵，我方的處境悽涼。我們的人多半已經捐軀了！敵人似乎逐漸壯大。

Joanne : I want to run away.

我想要逃走。

Leader : Run to where?

逃到哪兒？

Joanne : Safety?

安全的地方？

Leader : Then all of this will have been for nothing.

這樣一來，一切的努力都白費了。

Joanne : I'm too scared.
我怕死了。

Leader : Only the darkest times will **enlighten** us.
只有最黑暗的時刻可以帶給我們光明。

Joanne : What should I do?
我該怎麼做？

Leader : Look fear straight in the face and fight.
正視恐懼，並勇敢對抗。

With that, her leader ran into the battle and disappeared.
說完，她的領袖步入戰場消失蹤影。

Joanne : Wait!
等等！

All of a sudden Joanne sat up and she was in her room. Julie came running in.
瓊安突然坐起身，她在房間裡。茱莉跑了進來。

Julie : Are you okay? I heard you **screaming**.
你還好吧？我聽到尖叫聲。

Joanne : I had a dream.
我做了一個夢。

Julie　　: A **nightmare**?
惡夢嗎？

Joanne : No, it was a good dream.
不，是個好夢。

Julie　　: Are you sure you're okay?
你確定你還好？

Joanne : Yes.
對。

Julie said good night and closed the door. Joanne lay down with a smile on her face. She had the answer now.
茉莉向她道晚安，並把門關上。瓊安面帶微笑，躺了下來。現在她已經有了答案。

Keywords 聽力關鍵字

☑ **switch off**　　　　　　　　　　　　關上

☑ **ceiling**　　　　　　　　　　　　　天花板

☑ **clearing**　　　　　　　　　　　　空地

☑ **to be in shock**　　　　　　　　　震驚的

☑ **scream**　　　　　　　　　　　　尖叫

☑ **in the distance**　　　　　　　　　遠處

☑ thunderous	轟隆響的
☑ hoof	蹄
☑ battlefield	戰場
☑ clasp	緊握
☑ sword	劍
☑ suit of armor	盔甲裝
☑ bleak	悽涼的
☑ enemy	敵人
☑ enlighten	啟發；照亮
☑ nightmare	惡夢

MEMO

....

....

....

....

....

....

....

....

Questions 聽力關鍵題

1. _____

Ⓐ In her bedroom.
Ⓑ On a horse.
Ⓒ In the battlefield.
Ⓓ In Julie's room.

2. _____

Ⓐ A sword.
Ⓑ The answer.
Ⓒ A new leader.
Ⓓ A scream.

Answers and Translations 聽力中譯與解答

1. Where was Joanne in her dream?
夢裡瓊安在什麼地方？

Ⓐ 在她的寢室裡。　　Ⓑ 騎在馬上。
Ⓒ 在戰場上。　　　　Ⓓ 在茱莉的房間裡。

2. What did the dream give her?
這場夢帶給她什麼？

Ⓐ 一把劍。　　　　　Ⓑ 答案。
Ⓒ 一位新的領袖。　　Ⓓ 一聲尖叫。

答案：1→C　2→B

A New Day

新的一天

Start from here

The next morning, Joanne was up with the dawn and was cooking breakfast when Julie staggered into the kitchen. Julie was clearly tired, so Joanne made some coffee and then went to her room. She looked at the mess. Boxes of her things surrounded her. She hadn't unpacked yet. She smiled as she tore open the first box and began sorting through her things and hanging up her clothes. She heard the phone ring. Julie knocked on her door to tell her she had a phone call. Joanne went down the hall and picked up the receiver.

中譯

隔天，瓊安起了個大早。當茱莉跟蹌地步入廚房時，瓊安正在煮早餐。茱莉顯然很疲倦，所以瓊安煮了一些咖啡。然後她走回自己的房間，環視著房間的雜亂：好幾箱子東西圍繞著她；她還沒拆箱整理。她面露微笑，打開第一個箱子，開始整理她的東西，並將衣服吊好。她聽到一陣電話鈴聲，茱莉敲門說是找她的。瓊安走到走廊，接起電話。

🎁 Dialog 聽力對話

Joanne : Hello?
喂？

Mom : Hi, sweetie. It's Mom.
嗨，親愛的。是媽媽。

Joanne : Hi Mom! How are you?
嗨！媽！你好嗎？

Mom : Actually, I'm doing pretty well. I've started a painting class.
說實話，我過得不錯。我去上繪畫課了。

Joanne : Really? Wow! That sounds great! How do you like it?
真的？哇！聽起來很棒！你喜歡嗎？

Mom : Oh, it's hard but I love it. It's a talent I didn't even know I had.
滿困難的，但是我很喜歡。這是我一直都沒發現到的才能。

Joanne : Guess we're both figuring out our hidden talents this week.
看來這個禮拜，我們都找到自己的潛能了！

Mom : Oh? What's your hidden talent?
哦？你的潛能是什麼？

Joanne : Bravery.
　　　　勇氣。

Mom : Oh, you've always been brave, Joanne.
　　　　瓊安，你一直都很勇敢呀！

Joanne : You think so?
　　　　你真的這麼認為？

Mom : Honey, you packed up your life and left everything you knew and moved to start afresh in a big city. That's definitely brave.
　　　　寶貝女兒，你打包行囊離開自己熟悉的環境，到大城市開拓新生活，這就很勇敢了。

Joanne : Really? I think that was the easy part. The hard part is sticking it out.
　　　　真的？我認為這部分倒還簡單，難的是堅持下去。

Mom : Are you finding it hard to stay there? You know you can always come back home.
　　　　你覺得待不下去了嗎？你知道，你隨時都可以回家的。

Joanne : I know. I think this is where I belong though, at least for now.
　　　　我知道。不過我想，目前，我是屬於這裡的。

Mom : Joanne, I just wanted to thank you for what you've done for me.
　　　　瓊安，我也想感謝你為我做的一切。

Joanne : What do you mean?

什麼意思？

Mom : Well, you've **pushed** me to do things I was afraid of doing. Taking this class is a really big step for me.

嗯，你促使我去面對自己害怕的事。去上課，就是我跨出的一大步呢。

Joanne : Looks like I'm not the only one who's brave in the family.

看來我們家不是只有我勇敢呢。

Mom : No, I guess not.

嗯，應該吧。

Joanne : I better go, Mom. I've got a lot of **unpacking** to do. I love you.

不聊了，媽，我還有很多東西要整理呢！我愛你。

Mom : Okay, honey. I love you too. Keep in touch, little one.

好吧，乖女兒。我也愛你，要常連絡喔。

Joanne : Talk to you soon.

再見。

Joanne smiled as she hung up the phone and headed to her room to unpack.

瓊安面帶微笑地掛上電話，然後回房繼續整理東西。

Keywords 聽力關鍵字

☑	dawn	黎明
☑	stagger	蹣跚
☑	mess	凌亂
☑	surround	圍繞
☑	sorting	分類；整理
☑	hang up	掛電話
☑	receiver	聽筒
☑	hidden talent	潛能
☑	stick something out	堅持到底
☑	to push someone	促使某人
☑	unpack	打開（行李）

MEMO

....

....

....

....

....

....

....

....

Questions 聽力關鍵題

1. _____

Ⓐ Painting.
Ⓑ Bravery.
Ⓒ Taking a class.
Ⓓ Calling her daughter.

2. _____

Ⓐ Going to a new place.
Ⓑ Leaving her mother.
Ⓒ Unpacking.
Ⓓ Sticking it out.

Answers and Translations 聽力中譯與解答

1. What is Joanne's mother's hidden talent?
   瓊安媽媽的潛能是什麼？

   Ⓐ 繪畫。　　　　　Ⓑ 勇氣。
   Ⓒ 上課。　　　　　Ⓓ 打電話給女兒。

2. What is the hardest part of moving to a new city for Joanne?
   對瓊安而言，搬到新城市難在哪裡？

   Ⓐ 來到一個新地方。　Ⓑ 離開媽媽。
   Ⓒ 拆箱整理。　　　　Ⓓ 堅持到底。

解答：1→A　2→D

Chapter 2

Sarah Gets a Summer Job
莎拉暑假打工記

In this chapter, just take a quick look at each article, and then read along with the CD.

本章要訓練你：快速瀏覽過文章內容後，跟著 CD 一起唸，並作答。

Summer Vacation

暑假

Start from here

Sarah was relieved that school was finally over and that it was summer vacation. She looked forward to going to the beach, hanging out at the mall, and having a good time. When she found out that her favorite band, the Heartbreak Boys, were having a concert in her town, she knew it would be the best summer ever. She loved the Heartbreak Boys. She had pictures of them all over her bedroom. She even had a Heartbreak Boys pillow on her bed. Sarah had spent her allowance the day before on makeup and hairspray, so she needed to ask her Dad for the money to buy the concert ticket. She found her father in the kitchen and decided to ask him for an advance on her allowance.

中譯

　　學期終於結束了，莎拉的心情整個放鬆起來。趁著放暑假，她希望能到海邊去、逛購物商場，好好玩個過癮。得知她最喜歡的「心碎男孩」團體要到這裡開演唱會時，她相信這會是她記憶中最棒的夏天。她愛死「心碎男孩」了！她的房間貼滿他們的照片，甚至連枕頭都是「心碎男孩」。前天為了買化妝品和髮膠，她已經把零用錢花光了，所以她得跟老爸要錢買演唱會的票。爸爸在廚房，莎拉決定開口跟老爸預支零用錢。

 Dialog 聽力對話

Sarah : Hi, Dad. What are you doing?
爸，你在幹嘛？

Father : I'm just sitting here reading the paper and having a coffee. What's up?
我在這裡喝咖啡、看報紙，怎麼啦？

Sarah : Do you remember my favorite band, the Heartbreak Boys?
你記得我最喜歡的「心碎男孩」嗎？

Father : How could I forget?
我怎麼可能忘得了？

Sarah : They're having a **concert** here in town next month, and I just have to go!
他們下個月要來這裡開演唱會，我一定要去！

Father : So buy a ticket.
那就去買票啊。

67

Sarah : I can't. I ran out of money.
不行，我沒錢。

Father : Already! I just gave you your allowance yesterday.
這麼快！我昨天才發零用錢給你。

Sarah : I know, but I didn't hear about the concert until today! Is there anyway I can get an advance on my allowance.
我知道，但是我今天才知道他們要來啊！我可以預支下次的零用錢嗎？

Father : Another advance? No, Sarah. You are going to have to learn to spend your money more wisely.
又要預支？不行，莎拉，你要學會善用金錢。

Sarah : But Dad! I just have to go! If I don't, I'll die!
但是爸爸，我一定要去！不去，我會死！

Father : No one has ever died from missing a rock concert. I think you'll survive.
不去搖滾演唱會，死不了人的。我確定你會活下來的。

Sarah : This is horrible. I'll never get over this. I'll be scarred for life!
太可怕了，我會沮喪一輩子，這會是我一生的陰影！

Father : Sarah, don't be ridiculous. If it's that important to you, you'll just have to get a summer job.

莎拉，不要那麼誇張。如果這真的那麼重要，你就去打工啊。

Sarah : This is going to be the worst summer ever!

這會是個爛透了的夏天！

Keywords 聽力關鍵字

☑ summer vacation	暑假
☑ hang out	閒晃
☑ mall	大型購物商圈
☑ concert	演唱會
☑ hairspray	髮膠
☑ allowance	零用錢
☑ advance	預支
☑ ridiculous	荒謬的
☑ horrible	可怕的
☑ survive	生存
☑ important	重要的
☑ worst	最壞的

Questions 聽力關鍵題

1. _____

Ⓐ She asked him to buy her some makeup and hairspray.
Ⓑ She asked him to drive her to the mall.
Ⓒ She asked him for an advance on her allowance.
Ⓓ She asked him for advice.

2. _____

Ⓐ A ticket to the concert.
Ⓑ Some milk from the store.
Ⓒ An accountant.
Ⓓ A summer job.

Answers and Translations 聽力中譯與解答

1. What did Sarah ask her father?
   莎拉向爸爸要求什麼？

   Ⓐ 她要爸爸買化妝品跟造型液給她。　　Ⓑ 她要他載她到大賣場去。
   Ⓒ 她要預支零用錢。　　　　　　　　　Ⓓ 她向他尋求一些建議。

2. What did Sarah's father tell her to get?
   莎拉的爸爸要她去找什麼？

   Ⓐ 演唱會門票。　　　　　　　　　　　Ⓑ 商店買來的牛奶。
   Ⓒ 會計。　　　　　　　　　　　　　　Ⓓ 暑期打工。

答案：1→C　2→D

The Interview

面試

Start from here

Sarah decided that she needed to get a summer job. She really wanted to go to the concert, and had no other way to buy the ticket. She didn't know where to look for a job, so her father told her to read the Help Wanted section of the newspaper. Almost every ad she saw asked for someone with experience. She began to get discouraged, until she found an ad that said "Fun in the sun. Advertising and sales. No experience necessary." Sarah liked the idea of fun in the sun, so she decided to call the telephone number in the ad. After a short discussion with the manager of the company, Sarah was asked to go for an interview. She found the company's office in a run-down building.

中譯

　　莎拉決定找一份暑期工，因為她真的很想去演唱會，而這是唯一買到票的方法。她不知道到哪找工作，所以爸爸要她找報紙的求職版，可是報紙刊登的工作機會，都要求要有相關經驗。正當感到灰心時，她看到一個寫著「快樂艷陽下，廣告及業務員，無經驗可」的廣告。莎拉很喜歡快樂艷陽下的感覺，所以決定打電話過去問問。經理和莎拉談了一會後，就請她去面試。去之後，莎拉發現那間公司的辦公室在一棟破舊不堪的大樓裡。

🎁 Dialog 聽力對話

Sarah : Hi, I'm here for an interview with Mr. Foster.
你好，福斯特先生叫我來面試。

Receptionist : Have a seat. He'll be **right with** you.
請坐，他馬上就來。

Mr. Foster : Hello, you must be Sarah. Come on into my office.
你好，你是莎拉吧。請到我的辦公室。

Sarah : Sure. Nice to meet you.
好。很高興認識你。

Mr. Foster : Have a seat. Did you bring a **resumé** with you?
請坐。你有沒有帶履歷表過來？

Sarah : Um, I don't have a **resumé**. I've never had a job before.
嗯，我沒有履歷表，因為我從來沒上過班。

| Mr. Foster | : | That's okay. Like the ad says, no experience is necessary. |
| | | 那沒關係。就像廣告上登的一樣，無經驗亦可。 |

| Sarah | : | That's great, because I really need this job. |
| | | 太好了，因為我真的需要這份工作。 |

| Mr. Foster | : | Excellent. That's what we like here : enthusiasm! Do you know anything about advertising? |
| | | 很好。我們需要的正是這股熱忱！你懂廣告嗎？ |

| Sarah | : | Not really. |
| | | 不太懂。 |

| Mr. Foster | : | Do you know what the most effective way of advertising is? Word of mouth. People believe something when they hear it from a friend. That's how we achieve such outstanding sales. |
| | | 你知道打廣告最有效的方法嗎？是口碑。人總是相信朋友口中說出來的話，那也是為什麼我們能有如此卓越的業績。 |

| Sarah | : | I'm not sure I understand. |
| | | 我不太懂你在説什麼。 |

Mr. Foster : Don't worry, we have an excellent training program. Oscar is waiting for you outside in the van.

別擔心，我們有非常好的新人訓練課程。奧斯卡正在外面廂型車等你呢。

Sarah : Who's Oscar? I don't know if I feel comfortable getting in a stranger's van.

誰是奧斯卡？我不要隨便進陌生人的車。

Mr. Foster : Do you want the job?

那你要這份工作嗎？

Keywords 聽力關鍵字

☑	**Help Wanted**	徵人啟事
☑	**experience**	經驗
☑	**discourage**	使人灰心
☑	**resumé**	履歷表
☑	**advertising and sales**	廣告及銷售
☑	**enthusiasm**	熱忱
☑	**effective**	有效的
☑	**comfortable**	舒服的
☑	**stranger**	陌生人
☑	**be right with someone**	馬上與……會合
☑	**outstanding**	卓越顯著的
☑	**training**	訓練

Questions 聽力關鍵題

1. _____

Ⓐ She looked for a job at her father's office.
Ⓑ She looked in the Help Wanted section of the newspaper.
Ⓒ She looked downtown.
Ⓓ She went to the employment office.

2. _____

Ⓐ Telemarketing.
Ⓑ Door-to-door advertising.
Ⓒ Word of mouth advertising.
Ⓓ **Outstanding** sales.

Answers and Translations 聽力中譯與解答

1. Where did Sarah look for a job?
   莎拉從哪兒開始找工作？

   Ⓐ 她爸爸的辦公室。　　　　Ⓑ 報紙的人事求職版。
   Ⓒ 市中心。　　　　　　　　Ⓓ 她到就職中心去。

2. What did Mr. Foster say was the most effective form of advertising?
   佛斯特先生說最有效的廣告是什麼？

   Ⓐ 遠距行銷。　　　　　　　Ⓑ 挨家挨戶廣告。
   Ⓒ 口碑。　　　　　　　　　Ⓓ 卓越業績。

答案：1→B　2→C

Track-14

Start from here

Mr. Foster led Sarah to the large van outside the building. She was introduced to Oscar, who was the driver of the van. Mr. Foster explained that Oscar was going to train her in the field of advertising and sales. When Sarah entered the van she was relieved to find that there were five other people already there, and that she was not alone. She wasn't sure where she was going, or what she was supposed to do when she got there. She thought about the Heartbreak Boys, and decided that whatever it was, it would be worth it. Soon the van pulled into the local mall parking lot. Oscar stopped the van and told everyone to get out and get ready to enter the exciting world of advertising and sales.

中譯

　　佛斯特先生帶莎拉到外面的一輛長廂型車,然後將她介紹給司機奧斯卡認識。佛斯特告訴莎拉,奧斯卡會教她如何做廣告和銷售。進入車內後,她才感到放心,因為她不是單獨一個;車裡還有五個人。她不知道會被帶到哪裡,也不知道到了目的地後要做些什麼。但一想到「心碎男孩」,她就覺得一切都很值得。車子很快到一座購物中心的停車場。奧斯卡停了車，叫大家下車，準備進入刺激的推銷世界。

 Dialog 聽力對話

Oscar	:	All right, team! Are you ready to get out there and make some money!
		各位團員，準備好要賺錢了嗎？

Everyone	:	Yeah!
		準備好了！

Oscar	:	**Super**! Do you want to know what the most effective way of advertising is?
		讚！你們想知道什麼是最有效的廣告嗎？

Everyone	:	Yeah!
		想！

Oscar	:	Do you want to know how you can **achieve** the highest sales?
		你們想知道怎麼做出最高的業績嗎？

Everyone	:	Yeah!
		想！

Oscar	:	I'll tell you. Word of mouth advertising!
		我跟你們說，那就是以口碑來打廣告！

Everyone	:	What?

啊？

Oscar	:	Word of mouth! You know — when it comes directly from a person. That's how you **achieve** the highest sales, and make the most money!

口碑！就是從一個人口中直接說出來的話，也就是你達到最高銷售業績及賺最多錢的方法。

Sarah	:	What are we selling?

我們要賣什麼？

Oscar	:	We are selling the highest **quality**, most **decadent chocolate bars** on the market today. Believe me, these things almost sell themselves.

我們要賣的是高品質、目前市場上最高級的巧克力棒。相信我，這種東西大家搶著要買。

Sarah	:	Are we working in one of the stores here in the **mall**?

我們要在商場裡的店裡賣嗎？

Oscar	:	**Not exactly**. We work in a lot of different **locations** — that's why we have the van. We work outside! You know, fun in the sun!

沒有。我們要到很多不同的地方去賣，這就是要開廂型車出來的原因。我們是在外面跑生意的！所以才叫歡樂艷陽下！

Sarah	: We have to sell chocolate bars to people here in the parking lot?

我們要賣巧克力給停車場的人？

Oscar	: Exactly! Okay everybody, come and grab a bag of chocolate bars.

沒錯！好，現在大家各來拿一袋巧克力。

Keywords 聽力關鍵字

☑ introduce	介紹
☑ relieved	安心
☑ parking lot	停車場
☑ super	超級；讚
☑ outside	外頭
☑ achieve	達到
☑ explain	解釋
☑ mall	大型購物中心
☑ quality	品質
☑ decadent	高級豪華的
☑ not exactly	不盡然
☑ location	地點
☑ chocolate bar	巧克力條

Questions 聽力關鍵題

1. _____

- ❹ To be trained in the field of advertising and sales.
- ❺ To buy chocolate bars at the mall.
- ❻ To make friends in the parking lot.
- ❼ She wanted to go to the market.

2. _____

- ❹ In a store at the mall.
- ❺ In the exciting world of advertising and sales.
- ❻ In the market.
- ❼ In the shopping mall parking lot.

Answers and Translations 聽力中譯與解答

1. Why did Sarah get in the van with Oscar?
   莎拉為何進了奧斯卡的廂型車？

   ❹ 去接受廣告及銷售的訓練。　　❺ 去買大賣場的巧克力棒。
   ❻ 去停車場交朋友。　　　　　　❼ 她想去超市。

2. Where did Sarah have to sell chocolate bars?
   莎拉得在哪賣巧克力棒？

   ❹ 在大賣場的商店裡。　　　　　❺ 在傳銷的瘋狂世界裡。
   ❻ 在超市。　　　　　　　　　　❼ 在大賣場的停車場。

答案：1→A　2→D

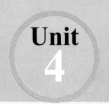
A Lucky Break

偷得浮生半日閒

Start from here

        Sarah did not want to sell chocolate bars in a shopping mall parking lot. It was not her idea of fun in the sun. She approached a few people leaving the mall, but no one would buy a chocolate bar. Some people got very angry and rude, which hurt Sarah's feelings. It was hot on the asphalt and the chocolate bars were melting from the heat. When a security guard told her that she did not have permission to sell on the shopping mall's property, she was happy to leave. She kept the bag of chocolate bars and walked to the nearest bus station. When Sarah got on the bus to go home, she spotted a cute guy sitting by himself. She sat down next to him and hoped that he would say hi.

中譯

        莎拉不想在購物中心的停車場賣巧克力。那跟她所想的「快樂艷陽下」完全不同。她走向一些要離開購物中心的人，試著賣巧克力給他們，但卻沒人要買。有些人不但對她生氣而且還非常地無禮，這讓她很傷心。柏油路很熱，巧克力棒都熔化了。當警衛告訴她，未經許可不准在商場的土地上兜售，她聽了很高興。她帶走整袋巧克力，往最近的公車站走去。當莎拉上公車準備回家時，她看到一位可愛的男生一個人坐。她坐到他旁邊，希望他能先開口打招呼。

🎁 Dialog 聽力對話

Trevor : Hungry?
餓了嗎？

Sarah : **Pardon me**?
你說什麼？

Trevor : That's one big bag of chocolate bars!
你手裡拿著一整袋的巧克力！

Sarah : Oh right! It's a long story. Do you want one?
對啊！說來話長，你要一條嗎？

Trevor : Sure! So, what's the story?
好啊！那麼，到底是怎麼回事？

Sarah : I need to get a summer job, but selling **overpriced** chocolate bars to angry people in a parking lot is not my idea of fun.
我需要一份暑期工，但是賣高價巧克力，給愛生氣的人，並不是件好玩的事。

When the security guard asked me to leave, I decided to keep the chocolate bars as payment for a day's work.

當警衛趕我走時，我決定自己留著這些巧克力，當做一天的酬勞。

Trevor : Ha! Summer jobs are boring. Why don't you just chill out for the summer?

哈！暑假打工很無聊的。你為何不輕輕鬆鬆地放暑假呢？

Sarah : I need money so I can go to the Heartbreak Boys concert. They're my favorite band.

我要賺錢去看「心碎男孩」的演唱會。他們是我最喜歡的樂團。

Trevor : No way! They're my favorite band too! What a coincidence! I was supposed to go with a friend, but he got into a car accident.

不會吧！他們也是我最喜歡的樂團！真巧！我本來準備跟一位朋友去的，但他出了車禍。

He's going to be in the hospital for a while and can't use his ticket. You can have his ticket for free, if you'd like to come to the show with me.

他必須住院一段時間，所以用不到票。如果你要跟我一起去的話，我可以把他的票送給你。

Sarah : Are you kidding? A free ticket! Of course I want to go!

你不是在開玩笑吧？免費的票！我當然要去囉！

83

Trevor : Okay. I'm Trevor, here's my phone number, call me next week and we'll arrange to go together. I have to go now. This is my stop!

那好，我叫崔維，這是我的電話。下禮拜打個電話給我，然後我們再約時間一起去。我要下車了。我到站了！

Sarah : Thanks! I'm Sarah. I'll call you next week.

謝了！我叫莎拉，我下禮拜再打電話給你。

Keywords 聽力關鍵字

☑	approach	走向；接近
☑	rude	無禮的
☑	asphalt	柏油
☑	melt	融化
☑	security guard	安全警衛
☑	permission	允許
☑	property	產業
☑	boring	無聊的
☑	overpriced	標價過高的
☑	chill out	放輕鬆
☑	arrange	安排
☑	coincidence	巧合
☑	free	免費的

Questions 聽力關鍵題

1. _____

Ⓐ She was hungry.
Ⓑ They were of the highest quality.
Ⓒ She considered it payment for a day's work.
Ⓓ She was angry and rude.

2. _____

Ⓐ The Heartbreak Boys are his favorite band.
Ⓑ His friend got into a car accident, and can't use the ticket.
Ⓒ He bought an extra one.
Ⓓ He sold the most chocolate bars.

Answers and Translations 聽力中譯與解答

1. Why did Sarah keep the chocolate bars?
   為什麼莎拉把巧克力棒留著？

   Ⓐ 她餓了。　　　　　　　Ⓑ 這是最高級的巧克力棒。
   Ⓒ 她認為這是她辛苦一天的報酬。　Ⓓ 她很生氣且粗魯。

2. Why did Trevor have a free ticket to the concert?
   為什麼崔維有免費的演唱會門票？

   Ⓐ 「心碎男孩」是他最愛的樂團。　Ⓑ 他朋友出車禍，用不到門票。
   Ⓒ 他多買一張。　　　　　　Ⓓ 他賣出最多巧克力棒。

答案：1→C　2→B

The Missing Number

電話號碼不見了！

Start from here

Sarah was ecstatic. She couldn't think of anything better than a free ticket to the concert and a date with Trevor. Best of all, she no longer needed a summer job. Now she could relax and hang out at the beach with her friends. Everything seemed great, until she looked for Trevor's phone number. It was nowhere to be found! Sarah was devastated. Suddenly everything seemed terrible. She had to find that phone number! Where did she see it last? Then she remembered that the last time she saw it was when she was with Trevor on the bus. She must have left it there! Sarah quickly grabbed her hat and coat and ran down to the bus stop. She waited anxiously for the same bus she had been on last week with Trevor. When it arrived, she rushed up the steps to speak with the driver.

中譯

　　莎拉簡直高興極了。她心想，沒什麼比免費的演唱會票，以及與崔維約會還好的事。最棒的是，她不必打工了。現在她的心情總算可以放鬆，還可以跟朋友一起到海邊玩。一切似乎很美妙，直到她要找崔維的電話號碼時，電話號碼不見了！莎拉很絕望，突然一切都糟透了。她必須找到他的電話號碼！最後在哪兒看到紙條的？她記得最後一次看到它，是和崔維在公車上的時候。她一定是掉在公車上！莎拉很快地拿起她的帽子和外套，然後跑到公車站去。她焦急地等上禮拜和崔維一起搭的那班公車。當公車到站時，她立刻衝上去問公車司機。

Dialog 聽力對話

Sarah : Hi there.
　　　　你好。

Bus Driver : Two dollars, please.
　　　　　　請投兩塊。

Sarah : Oh, I don't need to take the bus, I just need to take a quick look for something that I **lost** here last week.
　　　　喔，我不是要坐車，我只想快速找個上禮拜掉在車上的東西。

Bus Driver : Last week! Are you kidding me? We clean up these buses every night.
　　　　　　上個禮拜！你在說笑吧？我們每晚都會清理車子。

Sarah : You don't understand! I need to find it! It's a matter of life or death!

你不懂！我一定要找到它！這是攸關生死的大事！

Bus Driver : What did you lose? A kidney?

你掉了什麼？一顆腎臟？

Sarah : Not exactly — I lost a phone number on a scrap of paper.

不是。我掉了一張有電話號碼的紙條。

Bus Driver : A phone number! Give me a break! Normally I'd tell you to check the lost and found, but a scrap of paper! I hate to tell you, but that phone number's probably at the bottom of a garbage bin right now!

電話號碼！饒了我吧！平常，我會叫你去失物招領處找看看，但只是一張紙條而已！我實在不想説，你那張紙可能在垃圾筒最底下啦！

Sarah : Can't I just have a quick look around? Please?

我可不可以很快地找一遍？拜託？

Bus Driver : No way! I have a bus schedule to keep. You've wasted enough of my time as it is! Now, two dollars please, or leave the bus!

不行！我要照時間表開車。你已經浪費我很多的時間了！要嘛就付兩塊車錢，不然就下車！

Sarah : All right! I'm going, I'm going!

好！我走，我走！

Keywords 聽力關鍵字

☑ ecstatic		高興的不得了
☑ suddenly		突然間
☑ anxiously		焦慮的
☑ lost		遺失
☑ devastated		絕望
☑ remember		記得
☑ kidney		腎臟
☑ scrap		一小張
☑ give me a break		饒了我吧
☑ garbage bin		垃圾桶
☑ schedule		行程表

MEMO

....

....

....

....

....

....

....

....

Questions 聽力關鍵題

1. _____

Ⓐ Her chocolate bars.
Ⓑ Her kidney.
Ⓒ Her hat and coat.
Ⓓ Trevor's phone number.

2. _____

Ⓐ At the bottom of a garbage bin
Ⓑ In the lost and found.
Ⓒ At the back of the bus.
Ⓓ In the phonebook.

Answers and Translations 聽力中譯與解答

1. What did Sarah lose on the bus?
   莎拉在公車上弄丟了什麼？

   Ⓐ 她的巧克力棒。　　　Ⓑ 她的腎。
   Ⓒ 她的帽子和外套。　　Ⓓ 崔維的電話號碼。

2. According to the Bus Driver, where is the phone number?
   公車司機覺得電話號碼在哪兒？

   Ⓐ 垃圾筒深處。　　　Ⓑ 失物招領處。
   Ⓒ 公車後面。　　　　Ⓓ 電話簿裡。

答案：1→D　2→A

爸爸的建議

Start from here

Sarah was back to square one. Without a date and a free ticket to the show, she needed another summer job. She went back home and checked the "Help Wanted" section of the newspaper. She quickly typed and printed off six cover letters and resumé. She made sure her appearance was neat and tidy before she delivered the six resumé in person. Sarah hoped that at least one of the six people would call her for an interview. She stayed nervously by the phone for the next two days but no one called her back. She was very upset, and anxious to find a job quickly. The Heartbreak Boys show was just two weeks away, and she would be heartbroken if she couldn't go to that concert. She asked her dad for advice.

中譯

　　莎拉又回到了原點,約會和免費的演唱會入場票全泡湯了。她必須找另一份暑期工。她回家翻報紙的「求職版」找工作,且很快地打了六份的自薦信及履歷表。然後她整理好儀容,親自遞送履歷。莎拉希望六家公司,至少有一家會打電話要她去面試。她坐在電話旁等了整整兩天的電話,然而

卻沒有半家回覆。她又難過，又心急的想找份工作。離「心
碎男孩」演唱會的時間只剩兩個星期，如果去不成演唱會的
話，她真的會心碎的。她轉而向爸爸尋求建議。

 Dialog 聽力對話

Father : How's the job search going, Sarah?
莎拉，工作找的怎麼樣啦？

Sarah : It's horrible! No one is even calling me back for
an **interview**.
真是糟透了！根本沒半個人打電話約我去面試。

Father : Don't get **discouraged**, Sarah. There are lots of
different ways to find a job.
莎拉，別灰心。還有很多方式可以找到工作的。

Sarah : What do you mean? I've been **responding** to all
kinds of ads in the local paper.
什麼意思？我找了報紙上所有徵人的公司。

Father : Not every job is advertised, Sarah. You have to
network.
並不是每家公司都會登報徵人的，你要四處去打聽。

Sarah : **Network**?
四處去打聽？

Father : Yes, network. You have to get out there and talk to people.

是的，四處去打聽。你必須出去問人。

Sarah : What do you mean?

什麼意思？

Father : Do you have any friends with summer jobs?

你有沒有認識什麼人暑假在打工的？

Sarah : Yes. I know a few people that are working.

有啊，我有幾個朋友在打工。

Father : Why don't you ask your friends if there are any job openings where they work?

你何不去問問他們工作的地方有沒有在徵人？

Sarah : Oh, that's a good idea. I'm going to ask my friend Roddy. He works at the movie theatre. That could be a cool place to work! I wonder if they let you watch movies for free?

哦，那倒是個好主意。我去問問我朋友洛迪。他在戲院打工，在那工作應該很有趣。不知道能否看免費的電影？

Father : Now you're thinking Sarah! Get out there and show some initiative. Some of the best jobs are unadvertised.

莎拉，你總算開竅了！快去吧，主動一點。有些好工作是不會登出來的。

Keywords 聽力關鍵字

☑	cover letter	自薦信
☑	appearance	外表儀容
☑	neat and tidy	乾淨整潔的
☑	deliver	遞送
☑	anxiously	焦慮地
☑	interview	面試
☑	discouraged	灰心
☑	respond	回覆
☑	job opening	工作機會
☑	network	四處打聽
☑	movie theatre	電影院
☑	unadvertised	沒登廣告的
☑	initiative	主動

MEMO

Questions 聽力關鍵題

1. _____

A She e-mailed them.
B She sent out six faxes.
C She delivered them in person.
D She mailed out six letters.

2. _____

A To check the "Help Wanted" section of the newspaper.
B To network.
C To go to the movies.
D To stay by the phone.

Answers and Translations 聽力中譯與解答

1. How did Sarah deliver the six cover letters and resumes?
   莎拉怎麼把六份履歷發送出去？

   A 她用電子郵件寄出。　　**B** 她傳真了六份出去。
   C 她親自送出去。　　　　**D** 她用郵寄的。

2. What was her father's advice?
   她父親建議什麼？

   A 查詢報紙的「求職版」。　　**B** 四處打聽。
   C 去看電影。　　　　　　　　**D** 守在電話旁邊。

   答案：1→C　2→B

Start from here

Sarah was happy that she had talked to her dad. She hoped that one of her friend's employers were hiring. She went down to the muffin shop where her friend Judy worked, but the manager said that there were fully staffed. Next, she went down the block to the pet store where Samantha worked. After meeting the owner and smelling the pet store, she was happy that they were not hiring at this time. When she got home she called her friend Roddy who worked at the movie theatre. Roddy said that they were looking for people to work in the concession, serving drinks and popcorn. He said to go down to the movie theatre tomorrow and ask for Mr. Wilson, the manager. The next day Sarah did exactly that.

中譯

　　莎拉很高興有跟爸爸談過。她希望朋友的雇主們還有在徵人。她到朋友裘蒂工作的鬆餅店問，可是那家店的經理說他們已經額滿了。後來，她再到朋友莎曼珊工作的寵物店，見識過老闆與寵物店的味道後，她暗自慶幸他們現在不缺人。回到家後，她打電話給在戲院工作的朋友洛迪。洛迪說他們賣飲料及爆米花的販賣部有缺人，他叫莎拉明天到戲院找經理威爾森先生。莎拉隔天就去了。

 # Dialog 聽力對話

Sarah : Hi there, are you Mr. Wilson?
請問您是威爾森先生嗎？

Wilson : I sure am! How can I help you?
正是！有什麼事嗎？

Sarah : Hi Mr. Wilson, I'm Sarah. I spoke to my friend Roddy, and he said that you were hiring.
您好，我叫莎拉。我的朋友跟我說，您這裡正在徵人。

Wilson : Why yes, we are. We're looking for someone to work in the **concession** selling **popcorn**, candy, and drinks. It can get quite busy, so you have to be **fast on your feet**. Did you bring a resumé?
噢，沒錯。我們販賣部正缺一位賣爆米花、糖果及飲料的人。有時候會很忙，所以手腳動作要快。你有帶履歷表嗎？

Sarah : Yes I did. Here you are.

有，在這裡。

Wilson : I see that you don't have any work experience. What **skills** do you have that you can bring to the job?

看來，你一點工作經驗都沒有。你覺得自己為何適任這份工作？

Sarah : I'm a quick learner, Mr. Wilson. I'm also friendly and **courteous**. I think I would be good with the **customers**.

威爾森先生，我學得很快，而且態度友善、有禮貌。我也很會招呼客人。

Wilson : Very good! **Customer service** is very important. We had to let the last person go because he was too busy eating the candy to serve it to the customers!

很好！服務顧客是非常重要的。上個員工只顧吃糖而忘了服務客人，所以我們才請他走路的！

Sarah : Oh, I wouldn't do that.

喔，我不會這樣的。

Wilson : **Excellent**! You're hired!

非常好！你被錄取了！

Keywords 聽力關鍵字

☑ hire 徵人

☑ muffin 鬆餅

☑ manager 經理

☑ fully-staffed 員工額滿

☑ customer service 顧客服務

☑ popcorn 爆米花

☑ skill 專長；技能

☑ concession 販賣部

☑ fast on one's feet 手腳要快

☑ courteous 有禮貌的

☑ customer 顧客

☑ excellent 優秀的

MEMO

Questions 聽力關鍵題

1. _____

Ⓐ He is Roddy's father.
Ⓑ He works in the movie theatre concession.
Ⓒ He owns the pet shop.
Ⓓ He is the manager of the movie theatre.

2. _____

Ⓐ He wasn't fast on his feet.
Ⓑ He was too busy eating the candy to serve it to the customers.
Ⓒ He was always late.
Ⓓ He wasn't friendly or courteous.

Answers and Translations 聽力中譯與解答

1. Who is Mr. Wilson?
威爾森先生是誰？

Ⓐ 他是洛迪的父親。　　Ⓑ 他在電影院販賣部工作。
Ⓒ 他是寵物店的老闆。　Ⓓ 他是電影院的經理。

2. Why did Mr. Wilson let the last person go?
威爾森先生為什麼要辭掉上一個員工？

Ⓐ 他手腳不夠快。　　Ⓑ 他只顧自己吃糖，卻沒有服務顧客。
Ⓒ 他總是遲到。　　　Ⓓ 他不友善，也不禮貌。

答案：1→D　2→B

Unit 8

First Day at Work

上班第一天

 Track-19

Start from here

Things were looking up. Sarah was delighted that she had a summer job. Working at the movie theatre was cool — much better than selling chocolate bars in a parking lot! She hoped that she would get her first paycheck before the Heartbreak Boys concert sold out of tickets. If only she hadn't lost that phone number on the bus! She wished that she could go back in time when Trevor gave her his phone number and she had zipped it up safely in a pocket or purse. But since Sarah didn't have a time machine, she had to make do. She would have to work to buy her own ticket and hope to run into Trevor at the show. The next morning she went down to the movie theatre for a training session with Roddy.

中譯

　　事情進展得很順利。莎拉很高興找到了一份暑期工。在戲院工作遠比在停車場賣巧克力好的多了！她希望能在「心碎男孩」演唱會的票賣完前，領到她的第一份薪水。如果她沒有把電話號碼掉在公車上就好了。她真希望時間能夠倒流，那她一定會將崔維的電話號碼好好的放在袋子或是口袋裡，然後將袋口拉鍊拉好。因為莎拉沒有時光機，所以只好找份工作，自己賺錢買票，而且希望能在演唱會上碰到崔維。隔天，她到戲院跟著洛迪受訓。

🎁 Dialog 聽力對話

Roddy　：　Good morning, Sarah. Congratulations on getting the job! It's going to be fun working together.
　　　　　莎拉早！恭喜你得到這份工作！我們一起工作一定會很好玩的。

Sarah　：　Thanks, Roddy!
　　　　　謝了，洛迪！

Roddy　：　Here is your hat and name tag. The **uniform** is ugly, but the job has excellent **benefits**.
　　　　　這是你的帽子跟名片夾。這裡的制服雖然難看，但福利很好。

Sarah　：　There are **benefits**?
　　　　　有福利？

Roddy : Mr. Wilson likes you to be able to recommend movies to customers, so he lets his staff see movies for free.

威爾森先生希望你能跟客人介紹電影，所以他讓員工看免費的電影。

Sarah : That's awesome! I was hoping there'd be free movies.

那很棒！我就希望能看免費的電影呢。

Roddy : This is the cash register. It's very easy to operate. There's a button for every drink, candy or popcorn. Just press the buttons and it adds up the price.

這是收銀機，很容易操作的。飲料、糖果及爆米花都有各自的按鈕。只要按下按鈕，它就會自動加價。

Sarah : Do I get to make the popcorn?

我要做爆米花嗎？

Roddy : You sure do. This is where we keep the popcorn kernels. Empty a package of popcorn kernels into the popcorn maker once every ten minutes. Any questions?

當然要。這是我們放玉米粒的地方。每十分鐘把一包玉米粒倒進爆米花機裡就好了。有沒有疑問？

Sarah : When will I get my first paycheck?

什麼時候發薪水？

Roddy : We're paid on the first and fifteenth of every month.

每月的一號及十五號。

Sarah : The fifteenth! That's the day after the Heartbreak Boys concert!

十五號！那是「心碎男孩」演唱會的隔天啊！

Keywords 聽力關鍵字

☑ delighted — 高興的

☑ paycheck — 薪水

☑ zip up — 拉起拉鍊

☑ awesome — 太棒了

☑ uniform — 制服

☑ benefits — 福利

☑ button — 按鈕

☑ recommend — 推薦

☑ staff — 員工

☑ training session — 受訓期

☑ cash register — 收銀機

☑ operate — 操作

☑ kernel — 玉米粒

Questions 聽力關鍵題

1. _____

Ⓐ Free popcorn and candy when Mr. Wilson is not looking.
Ⓑ A good dental plan R.
Ⓒ Making popcorn every ten minutes.
Ⓓ Free movies.

2. _____

Ⓐ By pressing a button on the cash register.
Ⓑ By emptying a package of kernels into the popcorn maker.
Ⓒ Roddy makes the popcorn.
Ⓓ On the first and fifteenth of every month.

Answers and Translations 聽力中譯與解答

1. What are the benefits of working at the movie theatre?
在電影院打工的福利是什麼？

Ⓐ 威爾森先生不在時，就可以吃免費的爆米花和糖果。
Ⓑ 很好的牙齒保健。
Ⓒ 每十分鐘爆一次玉米花。　Ⓓ 免費的電影。

2. How does Sarah make the popcorn?
莎拉怎麼做爆米花？

Ⓐ 按一下收銀機。　　　　Ⓑ 把一包玉米粒倒進爆米花機。
Ⓒ 洛迪做爆米花。　　　　Ⓓ 每個月的一號跟十五號。

解答：1→D　2→B

Hard Work Pays Off

辛苦有了回報

Track-20

Even though she would miss the concert, Sarah still wanted to work at the movie theatre. She liked the benefits of free movies. She had fun working with her friend Roddy, and Mr. Wilson was a good boss. Sarah enjoyed serving the customers and making popcorn. After a couple of days of training, Sarah was an excellent employee. She was very quick on the cash register and always gave the customers the correct change. Sarah was always polite to the customers, even when some of them were impatient and rude. Mr. Wilson said that she was doing a great job and to keep up the good work. He liked that she always showed up on time, and that she didn't steal candy. One afternoon Sarah's father drove her to work, and asked her how her job was going.

中譯

　　雖然莎拉可能會錯過演唱會，她仍然想在戲院打工；她喜歡免費電影的福利，和洛迪一起工作很有趣，而且老闆威爾森先生人很好。莎拉很喜歡服務客人和做爆米花。才幾天，莎拉就成了一位很優秀的員工。她收銀很快，而且從未找錯錢。即使有些客人很沒耐性且粗魯，她對客人始終很有禮貌。威爾森先生說她做得很好，希望她能繼續保持。他也喜歡莎拉總是準時上班，又不偷糖果。有個下午，莎拉的父親載她去上班，並問她工作得怎樣。

 Dialog 聽力對話

Sarah　:　It's going great, Dad. I really like working there.
　　　　　爸，一切都很好。我真的很喜歡在那裡工作。

Father　:　I'm glad to hear that, Sarah. It's nice to see the work ethic you have developed.
　　　　　很高興聽你這麼說，莎拉。看到你的工作情操，讓我很欣慰。

Sarah　:　Thanks, Dad! Mr. Wilson says if I keep it up, I may be employee of the month.
　　　　　謝了，爸！威爾森先生說如果我繼續努力，可能會當選本月的模範員工。

Father　:　That's terrific, Sarah! I'm happy that you enjoy your job.
　　　　　很棒，莎拉！我很高興你喜歡你的工作。

Sarah : Yeah, it's fun. I'm glad I took your advice about networking.

是啊，工作很好玩，幸好我有聽你的話，請人幫忙打聽。

Father : Do you think you'll keep the job, even after you've bought your concert ticket?

那你買了演唱會門票後，還要繼續工作嗎？

Sarah : I won't get paid in time to buy a ticket. But I like my job, so I think I'm going to keep working part-time during the school year.

等到發薪日，已經來不及買票了。不過我真的喜歡這工作，所以開學後，我應該會繼續留下來打工。

Father : You won't be able to buy a ticket? That's too bad. Since you've been working so hard, I'm going to help you. I'll put it on my credit card, and you can pay me back when you receive your first paycheck.

來不及買票？真糟糕。看你工作那麼認真，這樣吧，我先刷卡幫你買票，等你領薪水後，再還我錢。

Sarah : Thanks, Dad. You're the best!

爸，謝謝您。你是最棒的老爸！

Keywords 聽力關鍵字

☑ impatient   不耐煩的

☑ steal   偷竊

☑ terrific   很棒的

☑ work ethic   工作情操

☑ develop   發展

☑ employee   員工

☑ polite   有禮的

☑ advice   忠告

☑ credit card   信用卡

☑ receive   收到

MEMO

....

....

....

....

....

....

....

....

Questions 聽力關鍵題

1. _____

Ⓐ She was always polite.
Ⓑ She was rude and impatient.
Ⓒ She was too busy eating candy to serve them.
Ⓓ She gave them the wrong change.

2. _____

Ⓐ Quit her job.
Ⓑ Work full-time.
Ⓒ Continue working part-time at the movie theatre
Ⓓ Get a credit card.

Answers and Translations 聽力中譯與解答

1. How did Sarah treat the customers?
莎拉怎麼對待客人？

Ⓐ 她總是很有禮貌。　　Ⓑ 她粗魯又沒耐性。

Ⓒ 她光顧吃糖，沒空服務客人。　Ⓓ 她找錯零錢。

2. What is Sarah going to do after summer vacation?
暑假過後，莎拉打算做什麼？

Ⓐ 辭掉工作。　　Ⓑ 做全職員工。

Ⓒ 繼續在電影院打工。　Ⓓ 辦張信用卡。

答案：1→A　2→C

A Happy Ending

喜劇收場

Track-21

Start from here

The next day Sarah's father bought her a ticket to the concert. He even gave her some spending money so that she could buy a shirt or poster at the show. Sarah was delighted that she would be going to the concert after all. She was so excited that it was almost all she could think of. She was daydreaming about the concert at work, when all of a sudden the popcorn machine began to overflow. Popcorn was spilling everywhere! It went over the counter and onto the floor. Sarah had not been careful, and had added too many packets of popcorn kernels. She was very embarrassed, and her face turned bright red. She began to sweep up the popcorn when she heard a customer laughing. To her surprise, it was Trevor!

中譯

　　隔天，莎拉的父親買了張門票給她，他還給她一點零用錢，讓她可以在演唱會中買紀念 T 恤或海報。莎拉很高興最後還是可以去看演唱會，她興奮的滿腦子都是演唱會的事。工作時，她在作演唱會的白日夢，突然，爆米花機滿出來了！

爆米花灑得櫃檯、地板到處都是！因為莎拉不小心放太多包玉米粒進去。她覺得很糗，滿臉通紅。當她在掃地上的爆米花時，聽到一位客人在笑。令她吃驚的是，這個人竟然是崔維！

Dialog 聽力對話

Sarah : Hi, Trevor! What are you doing here?
嗨，崔維！你怎麼會在這裡？

Trevor : I'm taking my little brother to see a movie.
我帶我弟弟來這裡看電影。

Sarah : That's so nice! I was hoping I'd run into you.
那很好啊！我就希望能遇到你。

Trevor : Really? When you didn't call me, I assumed you didn't want to see me again.
真的？你沒打電話來，我還以為你不想見我了。

Sarah : Oh, no! That's not the case. I lost your phone number! I even went back to the bus and tried to look for it!
喔，不！不是啦。我把你的電話號碼弄丟了！我甚至還去那班公車上找！

Trevor : That's too bad. When I didn't hear from you, I **promised** my little brother I'd take him to the concert. He likes the Heartbreak Boys, too.

真是糟糕。因為你沒打電話來，所以我就答應帶我弟去演唱會了。他也很喜歡「心碎男孩」。

Sarah : Who doesn't like them? I like them so much I got my own ticket!

誰不喜歡他們？我太喜歡他們，所以自己去買了一張票！

Trevor : Awesome! Maybe we can still go together. That is if you don't mind my little brother **tagging** along.

太好了！或許我們還是可以一起去，當然如果你不介意我弟跟的話。

Sarah : I'd love to!

我很樂意！

Trevor : Great! I'll give you my phone number so that we can **arrange** to go together.

好極了！我給你我的電話號碼，我們可以約時間一起去。

Sarah : Why don't I give you my number this time? Don't lose it!

這次換我給你電話號碼吧？不要丟了！

Trevor : Thanks. I won't!

謝了，我不會弄丟的！

Keywords 聽力關鍵字

☑	spend	花（錢；時間）
☑	daydream	做白日夢
☑	overflow	滿溢出來
☑	spill	灑出
☑	embarrassed	困窘的
☑	sweep up	掃起來
☑	laugh	笑
☑	run into	碰到
☑	assume	以為
☑	promise	保證
☑	tag	緊跟
☑	arrange	安排

MEMO

Questions 聽力關鍵題

1. _____

Ⓐ The machine was broken.
Ⓑ Roddy was too busy daydreaming.
Ⓒ Sarah did not pay attention and added too many kernels.
Ⓓ Sarah added a packet of kernels every ten minutes.

2. _____

Ⓐ He wanted to see Sarah.
Ⓑ He was at the theatre with some friends.
Ⓒ He was also working there.
Ⓓ He was taking his little brother to the movies.

Answers and Translations 聽力中譯與解答

1. Why did the popcorn machine overflow?
   為什麼爆米花機器爆滿了？

   Ⓐ 機器壞了。　　　　　　　　Ⓑ 洛迪作白日夢疏忽了。
   Ⓒ 莎拉不小心倒太多包玉米粒進去。　Ⓓ 莎拉每十分鐘就倒一包玉米粒進去。

2. Why was Trevor at the movie theatre?
   為什麼崔維在電影院？

   Ⓐ 他想見莎拉。　　　　　　　Ⓑ 他跟朋友一起去看電影。
   Ⓒ 他也在那邊工作。　　　　　　Ⓓ 他帶弟弟去看電影。

答案：1→C　2→D

Chapter 3

Brenda in the Big City (Part I)
布蘭達在大城市（一）

After the training of chapter 1 and chapter 2, this chapter will be more challenging. Read each article along with the CD, and then try to listen to it on your own until you know most of it.

在第一、二章的訓練後，第三章就更有挑戰性了。跟著 CD 一起唸課文，最後不看文章，自己聽聽看，看看你是否可以聽懂大部分的內容。

Chasing the Dreams

逐夢之旅

Track-22

Start from here

Brenda grew up in a small town. She thought small towns were boring because nothing ever happened. She decided one day to move away from her small town and live in the big city. She thought this was a good decision because she wanted to be a performer. Brenda had always enjoyed acting and wanted to become a star. She knew that she would never be famous unless she left her town and chased her dream.

So Brenda packed up everything she had and put it in the car. Her car was so full that there was barely any room left for her. She said goodbye to her horse, Buckley. Then she said goodbye to her family. Her mom was crying because she was sad Brenda was leaving. Brenda told her not to worry, and that everything was going to be okay.

中譯

　　布蘭達是在小鎮長大的。她認為小鎮很無聊，因為總是沒有新鮮事。她決定有一天要搬離小鎮，到大城市生活。她覺得這是很好的決定，因為她想要成為表演者。布蘭達很喜歡演戲，而且有自己的明星夢。她知道除非離開小鎮去追逐夢想，否則她永遠也成不了名。

　　就這樣，布蘭達打包一切塞到車上，車子幾乎沒位置讓她坐了。她向她的馬兒芭克萊告別，然後向她的家人告別。布蘭達要走，讓媽媽難過的哭泣。布蘭達要她不要擔心，一切都會很好。

Dialog 聽力對話

Mom	:	It won't be the same without you here, Brenda. 沒有你，這裡就不一樣了，布蘭達。
Brenda	:	Mom, don't cry. I'll be fine. This is going to be great. 媽媽，別哭。我會過得很好的。一切都會很棒的。
Dad	:	Do you have enough gas in the car? 你車子的油夠嗎？
Brenda	:	Don't **worry**, Dad. I have enough. 別擔心，爸爸。油夠用。

Dad	:	What about money? Do you have enough money?

錢呢？你的錢夠用嗎？

Brenda	:	I think so. Stop **worrying**!

我想夠的。不要再擔心了！

Brother	:	Can I have your room?

我可以住你的房間嗎？

Brenda	:	You want my old room?

你要我的房間？

Brother	:	Well, you're not coming back, are you? Your room is bigger.

呃，你應該不會回來了吧？你的房間比較大。

Brenda	:	How's that for love? Sure. Take my room.

真是手足情深啊？好，房間給你。

Brother	:	Thanks. Good luck. Let me know when you're a movie star.

謝了。祝好運。當你成為明星時，要讓我知道。

Brenda	:	You'll be the first to know.

你會是第一個知道的人。

Dad	:	Well, you'd better get going. You have a long drive ahead.

好吧，該上路了。你要開很遠的路。

Brenda : Okay. I'm off. Mom, stop crying. I'll see you at Christmas.

好，我要走了。媽，別哭了。聖誕節見。

Mom : Okay. I'll see you at Christmas.

好。聖誕節見。

Keywords 聽力關鍵字

☑ **performer** 表演者

☑ **act** 演戲

☑ **star** 明星

☑ **famous** 有名的

☑ **chase a dream** 追逐夢想

☑ **barely** 幾乎沒有

☑ **worry** 擔心

MEMO

....

....

....

....

....

....

Questions 聽力關鍵題

1._____

Ⓐ To buy a new car.
Ⓑ To become a star.
Ⓒ To chase a star.
Ⓓ To live in the big city.

2._____

Ⓐ She packed her dreams in her car.
Ⓑ She packed her mother in her car.
Ⓒ She packed everything in her car.
Ⓓ She didn't pack anything in her car.

Answers and Translations 聽力中譯與解答

1. What did Brenda decide to do?
   布蘭達決定要做什麼？

   Ⓐ 買新車。　　　　　　Ⓑ 成為明星。
   Ⓒ 去追星。　　　　　　Ⓓ 去大城市居住。

2. What did Brenda pack in her car?
   布蘭達在車裡裝了什麼？

   Ⓐ 她的夢想。　　　　　Ⓑ 她的媽媽。
   Ⓒ 她所有的東西。　　　Ⓓ 什麼也沒有。

答案：1→B　　2→C

Unit 2

Brenda Bites the Bullet

布蘭達咬牙闖關

Start from here

After a few months, Brenda realized she didn't have much money left. She looked for different acting jobs, but no one would consider her because she didn't have enough experience. She realized that she was going to have to bite the bullet and get a real job. After thinking carefully about the kind of work she wanted, she realized a job as a waitress would be the best. If she worked in a restaurant or nightclub she could make a lot of money in tips, but also be flexible with work hours. The best place to look for a job like that was in the newspaper. After buying a paper and looking in the classifieds, Brenda called many of the restaurants advertising for waitresses to see if they were still hiring.

中譯

　　幾個月後，布蘭達發現剩下的錢不多了。她尋找各式的演出工作，但是沒有人考慮要她，因為她經驗不夠。她知道她必須咬緊牙關並找到一個真正的工作。仔細思考她想要哪種工作之後，她知道當一個女服務生會是最佳的選擇。因為在餐廳或夜總會工作，她可以賺很多小費，同時工作的時數也很彈性。要找這類工作，最好的途徑就是報紙。買了報紙並看了分類廣告後，布蘭達打了很多通電話給徵求女服務生的餐廳，看看是否他們仍在找人。

 Dialog 聽力對話

Manager : Hi, this is Clark's. Can I help you?
嗨，這裡是「克拉克餐廳」。有什麼事嗎？

Brenda : Hi, I was wondering if I could speak to the manager?
嗨，我可以和經理說話嗎？

Manager : Yes, this is the manager. Can I help you?
是的，我就是經理。需要什麼嗎？

Brenda : I'm calling about your ad in the paper. Are you still hiring waitresses?
我打來是想問報紙廣告的事；你們還缺女服務生嗎？

Manager : Yes, we are taking applications this week. Do you have any experience?

是的，我們這個禮拜開始接受應徵。你有相關經驗嗎？

Brenda : Well no, not really. But I am a fast learner.

呃，沒有，但是我學得很快。

Manager : Right. Well, this place moves pretty quickly. It gets crazy in here at lunch. I need someone with at least two years' experience.

好。不過這裡的步調很快，午餐時間忙的不得了。我要請的是至少有二年相關經驗的人。

Brenda : Oh, I see.

喔，我了解。

Manager : I have a vacancy for a dishwasher. No experience required.

我有一個洗碗工的職缺。不需要經驗。

Brenda : No offense, but I have a university degree. I don't want to be a dishwasher.

沒有冒犯的意思，不過我是大學畢業生。我不想做洗碗工。

Manager : Well sorry, I can't help you. Good-bye.

那麼就抱歉了，我也愛莫能助。再見。

Keywords 聽力關鍵字

☑ realize	了解
☑ consider	考慮
☑ experience	經驗
☑ bite the bullet	咬緊牙關
☑ waitress	女服務生
☑ nightclub	夜總會
☑ flexible	彈性
☑ tip	小費
☑ I was wondering...	我想知道……
☑ application	應徵
☑ newspaper	報紙
☑ classifieds	分類廣告
☑ no offense	沒有冒犯的意思
☑ vacancy	空缺
☑ dishwasher	洗碗工
☑ required	要求
☑ no offense	沒有冒犯的意思
☑ degree	文憑

Questions 聽力關鍵題

1. _____

Ⓐ She didn't want to be an actor anymore.
Ⓑ She liked to bite bullets.
Ⓒ She was running out of money.
Ⓓ She couldn't get a job with the newspaper.

2. _____

Ⓐ She was ugly.
Ⓑ She didn't have enough money.
Ⓒ She was too busy working at the restaurant.
Ⓓ She didn't have enough experience as an actor.

Answers and Translations 聽力中譯與解答

1. Why did Brenda want to look for a job as a waitress?
   為什麼布蘭達想要找份女服務生的工作？

   Ⓐ 她不再想要當演員了。　　Ⓑ 她喜歡咬子彈。
   Ⓒ 她錢用完了。　　Ⓓ 她在報紙上找不到工作。

2. Why didn't anyone want to hire Brenda to be an actor?
   為什麼沒有人要雇布蘭達當演員？

   Ⓐ 她長的醜。　　Ⓑ 她錢不夠。
   Ⓒ 她忙著在餐廳工作。　　Ⓓ 她沒有足夠的演員相關經驗。

答案：1→C　2→D

Start from here

Brenda continued to look for work in a restaurant. After getting turned down by every restaurant she applied at, she realized she was going to have to get creative. She decided to add some restaurant work experience to her resumé. She didn't feel great about lying, but she knew she needed to do something — she was broke!

The next day Brenda found an ad in the newspaper that was just what she was looking for. The restaurant was brand new, high class and very expensive. She didn't think her chances were very good, but she knew she had to try. She got dressed up in some nice clothes and drove down to the restaurant.

When Brenda got to the restaurant she noticed that it had a great atmosphere. The décor was classy, tasteful and very comfortable. She liked the place immediately. She saw that many other people were applying for the same job. She filled out an application form and waited for her turn to talk to David, the manager.

中譯

　　布蘭達繼續找餐廳的工作。每次應徵每次碰壁的情況下，她了解到她必須要有些創造力。她決定在她的履歷裡加入一些餐廳工作經驗。她也不想說謊，但是她知道這樣下去不是辦法——她已經沒錢了！

　　隔天，布蘭達在報紙上看到一則中意的廣告。那間餐廳是新開的，相當高級，而且是高價位的。她知道錄取的機會不大，但是她也不得不試試。她穿上比較好的衣服，開車前往那間餐廳。

　　當布蘭達抵達時，她發現餐廳的氣氛很棒；裝潢別緻，有品味而且非常舒適，她立刻喜歡上這個地方。她發現應徵者很多。她填完了表格，等著跟經理，大衛面談。

🎁 Dialog 聽力對話

David : Brenda, take a seat here. Let's chat.
布蘭達，請坐。我們來聊聊。

Brenda : Okay. Thanks.
好的。謝謝。

David : Your resumé says you don't have much restaurant experience, but you do have a little.
你的餐飲相關經驗不是很多，但還是有一些。

Brenda : I worked at a restaurant in my hometown it wasn't as nice as this one though.
我在家鄉的餐廳工作過，不過它不像這間這麼高檔。

129

David : What do you know about fine wines and **delicate cuisine**?

你對美酒及精緻料理有什麼認識？

Brenda : Uh... nothing yet.

呃……還沒有什麼概念。

David : If you work in our restaurant, we expect you to be hard working but also knowledgeable about out menu items. Are you comfortable talking to people?

如果你在我們餐廳工作，我們希望你不只付出勞力，也要懂菜單上的東西。你可以自在地跟人談話嗎？

Brenda : Yes, of course. Actually I love talking to people.

當然可以。事實上，我很愛跟別人説話。

David : What are your future goals Brenda?

你的未來目標是什麼，布蘭達？

Brenda : You mean my goals while working here?

你是指我在這裡的工作目標嗎？

David : I'm assuming that your life dream is not to become a fine-dining **server**. What do you hope to do with your life?

我想你的夢想應該不是當一個高級服務生。你有什麼人生理想？

Brenda : I'm an actor. A few months ago, I packed up everything I had into my car and drove to this city.
我是個演員。幾個月前我打包一切，開車來這個城市。

I'm a very good actor, but no one will give me a chance. I need this job so that I can continue to live here.
我是一個很好的演員，但是沒有人要給我機會。我需要這份工作，讓我能繼續待在這裡。

David : Thank you for being honest with me. It wasn't too many years ago that I moved to this city for just the same reason.
感謝你的誠實。好幾年前，我也正是因為這個原因搬到這個城市來的。

Brenda : But if you're an actor why did you open this restaurant?
可是，若你是演員，為何要開這間餐廳？

David : I was an actor. I had some success with a few small roles, but eventually I realized that it wasn't what I wanted to do.
我曾經是個演員。我成功地演了幾個配角，但是最後我發現，這不是我想要做的事。

Brenda : And now you have your own restaurant, and you can be the star of this show.
現在你有了自己的餐廳，你就是自己秀場的主角了。

David : That's right.
沒錯。

Brenda : So will you take pity on me and give me a shot?

那麼，你會基於同情，給我一個機會嗎？

David : Well, I haven't told my partner Patrick yet, but between you and me... you're hired.

呃，我還沒和我的伙伴派屈克說，但是先跟你講個秘密……你被錄取了。

Brenda : Oh, thank you! You won't be sorry.

噢，謝謝你！你不會後悔的。

Keywords 聽力關鍵字

☑ turn down	拒絕
☑ creative	有創造力的
☑ resumé	履歷
☑ broke	破產
☑ atmosphere	氣氛
☑ décor	裝潢
☑ tasteful	有品味的
☑ chat	聊天
☑ delicate cuisine	精緻料理
☑ server	侍者
☑ take pity on	同情
☑ give someone a shot	給人機會

Questions 聽力關鍵題

1. _____

ⓐ She needed to buy more newspapers.
ⓑ She had to break something.
ⓒ She needed to dress up in nice clothes.
ⓓ She needed to lie on her resumé.

2. _____

ⓐ It was high-class, old and expensive.
ⓑ It was very expensive and comfortable.
ⓒ It had a great atmosphere and was very cheap.
ⓓ It was empty and nobody was there.

Answers and Translations 聽力中譯與解答

1. What did Brenda need to do to get a job?
布蘭達為了得到工作必須做什麼？

  ⓐ 她必須買更多報紙。   ⓑ 她必須打破某件東西。
  ⓒ 她必須盛裝打扮。   ⓓ 她必須在履歷上說謊。

2. Choose the answer that best describes the restaurant.
選擇一個形容那間餐廳最好的答案。

  ⓐ 它高級、古老且昂貴。   ⓑ 它昂貴且舒適。
  ⓒ 它氣氛絕佳且非常便宜。   ⓓ 它是空的且沒有人在那裡。

答案：1→D 2→B

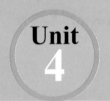

Unit 4

Wine School
品酒課程

🔘 Track-25

Start from here

Brenda was really excited about her new job. She felt relieved that she had solved her money worries. She bought some new clothes for her job, a blue button-up blouse and black pants. She also borrowed some books from the library about fine wines and dining. She wanted to study a little bit before she went to the first staff meeting. David had told her that at the staff meeting the entire staff was going to get a lesson about different wines and she wanted to be prepared.

Brenda felt it was a good time to call home. Finally she had some good news to tell her folks. She was tired of calling home to tell her parents she was running out of money and didn't have a job. She knew that this call would be welcome news.

中譯

　　布蘭達對她的新工作感到很興奮。因為金錢危機解除，讓她感覺很放心。她為了工作買了新衣服：藍色前扣上衣和黑色的褲子，她也從圖書館借了關於精緻飲食的書籍。她希望在第一次員工會議前做點功課；大衛說在員工會議中，所有的員工都會上一堂酒類的課程。她想要先預習。

　布蘭達覺得這是打電話回家的好時機，終於她有好消息可以跟家人分享。她已經厭倦了打電話回家卻只能說沒錢、沒工作。她知道這通電話正是大家期待的消息。

 Dialog 聽力對話

Brother ： Hello?
喂？

Brenda ： Hey Matt, how are you?
嗨，麥特，你好嗎？

Brother ： Same old, same old.
老樣子囉。

Brenda ： How's my horse? Have you been riding her for me?
我的馬呢？你有幫我騎出去嗎？

Brother ： I've been taking her out. I think she misses you, though. Did you call to ask me about your horse?
我固定會帶她出去晃晃。不過，我覺得她很想你。你專程打電話來問馬的事？

Brenda ： No, I have good news! I got a job.
不是，我有好消息！我找到工作了。

Brother : On a movie?

拍電影的？

Brenda : Well, I guess my news isn't that good. I got a job in a fancy restaurant called Bricks. I have my first **staff meeting** tomorrow.

嗯，還沒那麼好。我在一家叫「布克司」的高級餐廳，找到工作了。明天就是我的第一次員工會議。

Brother : Well, that's great, but what about acting?

嗯，那很棒，但是演戲呢？

Brenda : I have to pay the bills somehow.

我有帳單壓力呀。

Brother : I guess so. When is your first day on the job?

我猜也是。你什麼時候開始上班？

Brenda : I don't start for a couple of weeks. First I have to go to wine school.

還要幾個禮拜才能正式上陣。我要先上酒的課程。

Brother : That doesn't sound so bad.

聽起來不錯。

Brenda : I hope not. I have to learn all the **details** about fine wines and how to **pair** them with food.

希望如此。我必須學習美酒的明細，以及如何和食物搭配。

Brother	:	But do you get to drink the wine?
		那你會喝酒嗎？

Brenda	:	I guess so. The boss says it's important to understand the taste of different wines.
		應該會吧。老闆說了解酒的風味是很重要的。

Brother	:	Hmm. Maybe I'd like to go to wine school.
		嗯。我也滿想上美酒課程的。

Brenda	:	Maybe you should wait till you're old enough to drink first.
		你應該等到可以喝酒的時候再說。

Brother	:	**Details**, **details**.
		細節，細節。

Keywords 聽力關鍵字

☑ **relieved** — 放心；解脫的

☑ **solve** — 解決

☑ **blouse** — 女上衣

☑ **borrow** — 借

☑ **staff meeting** — 員工會議

☑ **entire** — 全部的

☑ **pair** — 配對

☑ **detail** — 細節

Questions 聽力關鍵題

1. _____

Ⓐ She bought some black pants and a blouse.
Ⓑ She bought some books on fine wines and dining.
Ⓒ She bought some lessons on wine.
Ⓓ She didn't buy anything for her job.

2. _____

Ⓐ She felt it was a good time to buy clothes.
Ⓑ She felt it was a good time to run out of money.
Ⓒ She felt it was a good time to go back to school.
Ⓓ She felt it was a good time to call home.

Answers and Translations 聽力中譯與解答

1. What did Brenda buy for her new job?
   布蘭達為了新工作買了什麼？

   Ⓐ 她買了黑褲子和一件女上衣。　Ⓑ 她買了一些精緻飲食的書。
   Ⓒ 她買了一些酒類課程。　Ⓓ 她什麼也沒有買。

2. What did Brenda feel it was a good time to do?
   布蘭達認為這是做什麼事的好時機？

   Ⓐ 她覺得是買衣服的好時機。　Ⓑ 她覺得是把錢花光的好時機。
   Ⓒ 她覺得是回學校的好時機。　Ⓓ 她覺得是打電話回家的好時機。

答案：1→A　2→D

Unit 5

The First Day on the Job

上任第一天

Track-26

Start from here

When Brenda arrived at the staff meeting she was introduced to her coworkers. Everyone was very nice. Some people were very new, just like her, while others had been working in the business for years. Brenda felt comfortable and hoped working with them would be fun. David the manager told everyone to sit down and take notes because the next week there would be a test on everything he talked about in the meeting. He introduced different areas of France, different kinds of grapes and different winemaking styles. Brenda didn't really think the lecture was very interesting but she did listen carefully. After David spoke for about an hour he informed everyone that the wine tasting would begin.

中譯

　　布蘭達到達員工會議時，她被介紹給她的同事們。每個人都很好。有些人也和她一樣是新人，有些人則在這一行做了很多年。布蘭達覺得很自在，並希望和大夥兒一起工作會很愉快。經理大衛要大家坐下來並作筆記，因為會議中他說的所有事情，下個禮拜會有一個測驗。他介紹法國的不同地區，不同種類的葡萄和不同的製酒方式。布蘭達並不覺得上課很有趣，但是她仍然很專心聽。大衛講了約一小時後，他宣佈馬上要開始品酒了。

 Dialog 聽力對話

David : All right everyone, does anyone know how to taste wine?

好，各位，有人知道要如何品酒嗎？

Girl : You drink it in little **sips**?

以小口啜飲的方式品嘗？

David : Yes, that's partly true.

沒錯，但只答對了一部分。

You must **swirl** the glass while smelling the **aroma**, then take a little wine in your mouth and **mix** it with air like this. That way you can get the full taste of the wine.

你要邊搖晃玻璃杯邊品味酒香，之後再淺嚐一口。先在口中與空氣混合後，再吞下，這才是完整的品酒步驟。

How would you describe this flavor to a customer?

你會怎麼跟客人描述這種酒？

Girl   : **Fragrant**, deep and **full-bodied**.

芳香，味沉且濃烈。

David   : That's great; do you know what it means?

很好；你知道這代表什麼嗎？

Girl   : Well uh no, but it always seems to **impress** customers.

呃，不知道，不過這樣說，客人比較會有印象深刻的感覺。

David   : Thank you for being honest, but I need you to do better than that.

謝謝你的誠實，但是我要的不只這些。

All right, let's have a few questions. Does anyone know what it means for a red wine to have "legs"?

好，大家一起來討論幾個問題。有人知道，有「腳」的紅酒是什麼意思嗎？

Boy   : It means someone drank the wine so fast it grew legs and walked away?

是說有人喝太快，所以酒長腳跑掉了？

David   : Interesting, but no.

很有趣，但不是。

Brenda : Doesn't "legs" mean wine dripping down the inside of the glass after you swirl it? Cheap wine doesn't have legs.

「腳」是不是說，酒在搖晃後滲入玻璃杯？便宜的酒不會有這種現象。

David : That's right, Brenda. Looks like you could have a knack for this.

對，布蘭達。看來你對這一門學問似乎滿有天份的。

Keywords 聽力關鍵字

☑	coworker	同事
☑	test	測驗
☑	style	型態
☑	lecture	講課
☑	sip	啜飲
☑	swirl	旋轉
☑	aroma	香氣
☑	mix	混合
☑	fragrant	芳香的
☑	full-bodied	濃烈的
☑	impress	印象深刻
☑	drip	滴下
☑	a knack for something	對什麼有本領

Questions 聽力關鍵題

1. _____

Ⓐ Brenda liked the meeting because they drank wine.
Ⓑ She thought the lecture was very interesting.
Ⓒ She didn't think the lecture was interesting.
Ⓓ Brenda felt like the meeting lasted years.

2. _____

Ⓐ There will be a test about the class.
Ⓑ They will all taste wine.
Ⓒ Brenda will go to France.
Ⓓ They will make wine.

Answers and Translations 聽力中譯與解答

1. What did Brenda think about the meeting?
布蘭達對會議有什麼想法？

Ⓐ 布蘭達喜歡會議因為他們喝酒。　Ⓑ 她認為講課很有趣。
Ⓒ 她並不認為講課很有趣。　　　　Ⓓ 布蘭達覺得像去年的會議。

2. What will happen next week?
下週將發生什麼事？

Ⓐ 將有一個課程的複習考。　Ⓑ 他們全部都將品酒。
Ⓒ 布蘭達將去法國。　　　　Ⓓ 他們將製酒。

答案：1→C　2→A

Unit 6
The Police
警察

Start from here

Finally, the staff meeting was over. Brenda was feeling a bit more relaxed because of the wine tasting. After she said good-bye to everyone she got into her car and started to drive home, thankful that her long day was over.

As Brenda drove home she was listening to the radio. When her favorite song came on, she began to sing along. She was singing loudly and not paying attention to the road, so it took her some time to notice a police officer waving to pull her over. When she finally did pull over, the policeman was very angry.

中譯

　　終於，員工會議結束了。品過酒後，布蘭達感覺放鬆很多。和大家道別後，她準備開車回家，慶幸辛苦的一天終於結束。

　　在布蘭達開車回家的時候，她一面聽著廣播。當她最喜歡的歌出現，她開始跟著唱。她唱得很大聲而沒有注意路況，所以她花了一點時間才注意到警察對她搖手要她靠邊停。當她終於把車開到路邊停下來時，警察先生非常生氣。

Dialog 聽力對話

Policeman : Don't you know when to stop when you see a policeman?

你不知道何時看到警察要停下來嗎？

Brenda : Well, I didn't know you wanted me to stop. Usually police don't stand in the middle of the road **waving** their arms like that.

呃，我不知道你要我停下來。通常警察不會像那樣站在路中間揮著手臂。

Policeman : Why didn't you **pull over** when I turned on the motorcycle lights?

為什麼在我打開摩托車燈時你不靠邊停？

Brenda : I did stop. I'm stopped right now aren't I?

我有停。我現在就停著了，不是嗎？

Policeman : Are you trying to **be smart with** me?

你是在我面前耍聰明嗎？

Brenda : No, I'm just answering your questions.

不，我只是在回答你的問題。

Policeman : Do you know how fast you were going?

你知道你剛才開多快嗎？

Brenda : Am I getting a ticket?

我要被開單了？

Policeman : Have you been drinking? I can smell **alcohol**.
你有喝酒嗎？我聞到酒味。

Brenda : I was just at a staff meeting; they asked us to taste some wine.
我剛才有一個員工會議；他們叫我們品酒。

Policeman : Step out of the car please, Miss.
請下車，小姐。

Brenda : I'm not **drunk**.
我沒有醉。

Policeman : Get out of the car now!
現在就下車！

Keywords 聽力關鍵字

☑ relax	放鬆
☑ favorite	最喜愛的
☑ attention	注意
☑ wave	搖；揮
☑ pull over	靠邊停
☑ alcohol	酒精
☑ be smart with	要聰明
☑ drunk	喝醉

Questions 聽力關鍵題

1. _____

Ⓐ She drank more wine and sang loudly.
Ⓑ She danced with the policeman to very loud music.
Ⓒ She started to drive home.
Ⓓ She had a date with a policeman.

2. _____

Ⓐ She was singing too loudly.
Ⓑ She was driving too fast.
Ⓒ She smelled like wine.
Ⓓ Her car lights weren't on.

Answers and Translations 聽力中譯與解答

1. What did Brenda do after her meeting?
布蘭達在她的會議結束後做了什麼事？

Ⓐ 她喝了許多酒且唱歌唱得很大聲。　Ⓑ 她以很大聲的音樂和警察跳舞。

Ⓒ 她開始開車回家。　Ⓓ 她和警察約會。

2. Why did the police office want Brenda to get out of the car?
為什麼警察要布蘭達下車？

Ⓐ 她唱歌太大聲。　Ⓑ 她開車開太快。
Ⓒ 她聞起來有酒味。　Ⓓ 她的車燈沒開。

答案：1→C　2→C

Billy's New Truck
比利的新卡車

Track-28

Start from here

After doing a few breath tests for the police officer, Brenda was allowed to go home. The policeman gave Brenda a speeding ticket, with a fine of 250 dollars. She drove to her apartment carefully and slowly. Now she had even more expenses. How was she going to get enough money? She couldn't even think about acting. She had too many bills to pay. She fell asleep with her clothes on. She was too tired to change.

The next morning when Brenda woke up she felt better. "I am finished with this pity-party," she thought to herself. "Today is my first day of work and I am going to do great." Just then the phone rang.

中譯

　　警察做了一些酒精測試後，准許布蘭達回家。警察開了一張二百五十元的超速罰單給布蘭達。她小心、慢慢地開回她的公寓。現在她的開銷更大了，她怎麼有足夠的錢？她連演戲都顧不到，因為有太多帳單要付了。她和衣就寢，因為她實在太累了。

　　隔天早上布蘭達醒來時，她覺得好多了。「自怨自哀也夠了，」她對自己說。「今天是我工作的第一天，而且我會做得很好。」此時，電話正好響了。

🎁 Dialog 聽力對話

Brenda ： Hello?
喂？

Billy ： Hey, it's me, Billy.
嘿，是我，比利。

Brenda ： Wow! Nice to hear from you. How are you?
哇！很高興聽到你的電話。你好嗎？

Billy ： Can't **complain**. What's new with you? Are you a big star yet?
還好。你近來怎樣？當成大明星了嗎？

Brenda ： Oh, not yet.
哦，還沒有。

Billy ： Well, there is always room for one more in Hollywood.
嗯，好萊塢永遠都容得下一個新人的。

Brenda : Ha! I'm sure. What's up with you?
哈！我確定。那你呢？

Billy : I bought a truck. I'm fixing it up. It's slow but it works.
我買了一輛卡車。我正在修理它，雖然慢但還可以開。

Brenda : How much was it?
多少錢？

Billy : Five cents.
五分錢。

Brenda : Wow. Expensive.
哇，好貴。

Billy : The funny thing is at the time I didn't even have a **nickel** in my **pocket**. I am not even worth a **nickel**.
有趣就在當時我口袋根本沒半毛錢，我根本不值幾個錢。

Brenda : I guess that guy didn't want that truck too badly.
那傢伙大概沒那麼想要那輛卡車吧。

Billy : No, I guess not.
嗯，或許吧。

Keywords 聽力關鍵字

☑	breath test	酒精測試
☑	allow	准許
☑	speeding ticket	超速罰單
☑	fine	罰金
☑	apartment	公寓
☑	expense	開銷
☑	carefully	小心
☑	pity-party	自怨自哀
☑	complain	抱怨
☑	pocket	口袋
☑	nickel	五分鎳幣

MEMO

....
....
....
....
....
....
....
....

Questions 聽力關鍵題

1. _____

🅐 She was thinking about acting.
🅑 She was busy doing tests.
🅒 She was too tired to change.
🅓 She had too many bills to pay.

2. _____

🅐 He bought a truck for five cents.
🅑 He bought a truck for $250.00.
🅒 He's moving to Hollywood.
🅓 He doesn't have any pockets.

Answers and Translations 聽力中譯與解答

1. Why did Brenda fall asleep with her clothes on?
   1. 布蘭達為什麼穿著衣服就睡著了？

   🅐 她想著演戲。　　🅑 她忙著考試。
   🅒 她累得無法換衣服了。　🅓 她有太多的帳單要付了。

2. What news did Billy tell Brenda?
   2. 比利告訴布蘭達什麼消息？

   🅐 他花了五分錢買了一輛卡車。　🅑 他花了二百五十元買了一輛卡車。
   🅒 他要搬去好萊塢。　🅓 他沒有任何的口袋。

答案：1→C　2→A

Unit
8

The Big Spill

打翻了！

 Track-29

Start from here

After a relaxed afternoon at home, Brenda got ready for her first big night at work. She put on her uniform, styled her hair and put on some makeup. She arrived at work with lots of extra time. She wanted everything to go smoothly. She didn't have to wait long before the place was filled with customers.

Brenda noticed these customers weren't exactly strangers. She knew who a lot of the people were. She recognized them from television and the movies! They had all finished working on a new movie. They were celebrating the end of filming. Brenda grew a little nervous. All this time in the big city and this was the closest she had been to the movie business. She felt excited that her first night at the restaurant would be so memorable.

Then something happened that Brenda would never forget.

She was carrying a tall glass of red wine. While crossing the floor, a man walked into Brenda. The wine splashed all over the man's pants. The man was furious.

中譯

　　在家裡休息了一個下午後，布蘭達準備好面對第一個重要的夜班。她穿好制服，梳個髮型，上了點妝。她提早到了餐廳，因為她希望一切進展順利。不久，餐廳就滿了客人。

　　布蘭達發現那些客人並不全然陌生，她知道大部分的人是何方神聖──從電視和電影上得知！他們都是新片剛殺青，來這裡慶祝的。布蘭達開始有點緊張。在大城市裡的所有時間裡，這次是她和電影事業最接近的時候。她因為第一夜輪班就如此難忘，感到相當興奮。

　　後來就發生了一件布蘭達忘不了的事。

　　她端著一只高腳杯裝的紅酒。穿過場地時，一位男士撞上布蘭達，他的褲子被酒濺到了。男士大發雷霆。

🎁 Dialog 聽力對話

Brenda ： I am so sorry.
真的很抱歉。

Man ： You better be sorry. You idiot!
最好是。你這個白癡！

Brenda ： Let me get a towel.
我幫您拿條毛巾來。

Man	:	Where is the manager? I will have your job. Red wine on white pants! These pants are ruined! 經理在哪？我要叫他炒妳魷魚。紅酒灑在白褲子上！這褲子毀了！

Brenda	:	I am sorry you are wearing white pants, sir. 很遺憾您今天穿的是白色褲子，先生。

David	:	Sir, can I help you? Is everything all right? 先生，有什麼事嗎？一切都還好嗎？

Man	:	No, everything is not all right! Look at me! 不，不好！你看看！

David	:	I am sorry sir, how can we make this up to you? 對不起，先生，我們該怎麼彌補您的損失？

Man	:	You can start by getting this stupid girl out of my face! 你可以先讓這個笨女生從我面前消失！

David	:	Brenda, why don't you go to the back for a five-minute break? I'll come and talk to you in a minute. 布蘭達，你到內場休息個五分鐘，好嗎？我一會兒後過去找你。

Keywords 聽力關鍵字

☑ style	設計
☑ uniform	制服
☑ makeup	化妝
☑ extra	額外的；空餘的
☑ smoothly	平順的
☑ stranger	陌生人
☑ celebrate	慶祝
☑ filming	拍片
☑ memorable	令人難忘的
☑ splash	潑；灑
☑ idiot	白癡
☑ ruined	毀壞的

MEMO

....

....

....

....

....

....

Questions 聽力關鍵題

1. _____

Ⓐ She watched a movie and drank some wine.
Ⓑ She put on her uniform and arrived at work early.
Ⓒ She waited a long time for a haircut.
Ⓓ She became very nervous and forgot everything.

2. _____

Ⓐ Brenda dropped food on the man's pants.
Ⓑ Brenda washed the man's pants.
Ⓒ Nothing happened to his pants.
Ⓓ Brenda splashed wine on his pants.

Answers and Translations 聽力中譯與解答

1. What did Brenda do to prepare for work?
布蘭達為工作做了什麼準備？

Ⓐ 她看了場電影並喝了一些酒。　　Ⓑ 她穿上制服並提早上班。
Ⓒ 她為剪頭髮等了很長一段時間。　Ⓓ 她變得很緊張且什麼事都忘了。

2. What happened to the man's pants?
那位男士的褲子怎麼了？

Ⓐ 布蘭達把食物灑在他的褲子上。　Ⓑ 布蘭達洗了他的褲子。
Ⓒ 沒有事發生。　　　　　　　　　Ⓓ 布蘭達把酒灑在他的褲子上。

答案：1→B　2→D

Track-30

Start from here

Brenda did as she was told. She waited in the kitchen to talk to David. She was upset. She was scared that she was going to lose her job. She was also angry because the man had been so rude to her. "He was the one who bumped into me," she thought. Every minute she waited was like an hour. She tried to sit still and be patient, but she couldn't. She wanted to know what was going on in the next room. She peeked through the doorway at David and the man. That man was very familiar to Brenda. "Who is that guy?" she thought. Then a light bulb went on in her head. "Oh my! That's Paul Jones, the famous movie director!" Now Brenda felt terrible. She would be fired for sure.

Brenda didn't have to wait much longer before David came back into the kitchen.

中譯

　　布蘭達照做了，她到廚房等著和大衛談話。她很沮喪，害怕會失去這份工作，也因為男士如此無禮的態度，讓她感到生氣。「是他撞到我的，」她想。等待的每一分鐘都很漫長，她想安靜坐著並保持耐心，但是她沒辦法。她想知道外場發生什麼事。她從門口偷看著大衛及那位男士。那個男人看起來很面熟。她想：「那個男的是誰？」然後她突然靈光一閃：「噢，我的天！那是保羅‧瓊斯，那個有名的電影導演！」現在布蘭達感覺大事不妙──她一定會被開除。

　　布蘭達並沒有等很久，大衛便回到廚房來了。

🎁 Dialog 聽力對話

David : Brenda, let's talk.
布蘭達，我們談一談。

Brenda : David, I am so sorry. He crashed into me. I didn't even see him.
大衛，我很抱歉。他撞到我。我根本沒看到他。

David : I know. I saw the whole thing.
我知道。我全部都看到了。

Brenda : You did? So I'm not fired?
你看到了？所以我不會被開除？

David : Fired? For that?
開除？為了那件事？

Brenda : But I spilled a drink on PAUL JONES! He is **huge**! I'm so embarrassed.

我把酒灑在「保羅・瓊斯」身上！他是大人物！我好丟臉。

David : Ah, don't worry about it. Before the night is over he'll be spilling drinks on himself. The guy is a drunk.

啊，不用擔心，晚宴結束前，他會自己把酒灑在身上。這傢伙是個酒鬼。

Brenda : Is he still mad?

他還在生氣嗎？

David : Nah, I gave him some free **booze**. I'm sure he has forgotten the whole thing.

沒啦，我請他喝點免費的酒。我確定他已經忘了整件事。

Brenda : That guy was so **rude** to me. I wanted to kick him.

那傢伙對我很不禮貌。我當時真想踹他。

David : I'm sure you did. I have one piece of **advice** when dealing with **rude** customers.

我知道，但針對無禮的客人，我可以給你個建議。

Brenda : What's that?

什麼建議？

David : Don't give them the fight they want. That's what they are looking for.

不要跟他們吵，因為這正稱了他們的意，這些人就是想找碴。

Imagine, that guy has a wife and kids somewhere. If he is that rude to a total stranger, imagine how he treats his family.

你想，那男的也是有家室的人了，如果他對陌生人都這麼無禮，你想他會怎麼對待他的家人？

Brenda : Good point.

有道理。

David : Be thankful we only have to experience him for one evening at a time.

要慶幸我們只需忍受他一個晚上。

Brenda : Well, now what? Should I go back out there?

嗯，那現在呢？我應該回到外場去嗎？

David : Well, I will leave that up to you. If you want to go home, I think we can handle it.

這就看你了。你要回去也可以，我想我們還忙得過來。

Brenda : I would rather stay and finish my shift.

我想留下來值完班。

David : OK, you work up front and stay clear of Mr. Jones.

好，那你回外場去，記得離瓊斯先生遠一點。

Keywords 聽力關鍵字

☑	kitchen	廚房
☑	patient	耐心
☑	peeked	偷看
☑	familiar	熟悉
☑	director	導演
☑	huge	巨大的
☑	booze	酒類飲料
☑	imagine	想像
☑	treat	對待
☑	shift	輪班

MEMO

Questions 聽力關鍵題

1. _____

Ⓐ She was scared to go into the kitchen.
Ⓑ She was scared she would lose her job.
Ⓒ She was scared because she doesn't like dark places.
Ⓓ She was very scared because David was angry.

2. _____

Ⓐ Don't give customers the fight they want.
Ⓑ Never wear white pants and drink red wine.
Ⓒ Be rude to your family and total strangers.
Ⓓ If people are angry give them free booze.

Answers and Translations　聽力中譯與解答

1. Why was Brenda scared?
布蘭達為什麼害怕？

Ⓐ 她害怕到廚房去。　　　　Ⓑ 她害怕她會丟掉工作。
Ⓒ 她害怕因為她不喜歡黑暗的地方。Ⓓ 她非常害怕因為大衛生氣了。

2. What advice did David give Brenda?
大衛給了布蘭達什麼建議？

Ⓐ 不要如他們所要的和他們爭吵。　Ⓑ 永遠不要穿白褲子喝紅酒。
Ⓒ 要對你的家人及陌生人無禮。　　Ⓓ 如果有人生氣了就給他們免費
　　　　　　　　　　　　　　　　的酒。

答案：1→B　2→A

Unit 10

The Man in Leather

皮衣男子

Track-31

Start from here

Brenda went back out into the party. Everyone was having a good time, even rude old Mr. Jones. Brenda's coworkers told her not to worry about what happened, which made her feel a lot better. The customers seemed to like Brenda a lot. There was one customer in particular who seemed to take a liking to Brenda. Brenda didn't think he was an actor because she didn't recognize him. There were some things she did notice about him though. He was a sharp dresser. He wore a black leather jacket, and leather boots. Brenda wondered who he was but knew it would be impolite to ask.

After a long night, it was finally closing time. Brenda did her cleaning duties then said good-bye to everyone. She left the building and walked to her car. She was glad her first day was over. Now she could go home and get some sleep.

Brenda was moving her car out of her parking space

when "Bang!" another car crashed into her.

Brenda jumped out of her car. A man dressed in leather stepped out of his.

中譯

　　布蘭達回到宴會裡。每個人都很開心，甚至是無禮的老瓊斯先生。布蘭達的同事要她別在意發生的事，這讓她感覺好多了。客人們都滿喜歡布蘭達的，其中一位似乎對布蘭達特別有好感。布蘭達不認為他是個導演，因為她不認識他。然而，她也發現這個人有個特色；他很會穿衣服。他穿著黑色的皮外套和皮靴。布蘭達想知道他是誰，但是她知道問這個問題並不禮貌。

　　經過這漫長的一晚，終於到關店的時間了。布蘭達完成了清潔工作後和每個人說再見。她離開大樓走向她的車子。她很高興工作第一天結束了。現在她可以回家睡一覺。

　　布蘭達正要把車開出來時，「碰！」的一聲，一輛車撞了上來。

　　布蘭達跳出她的車，一位皮衣男子也走下了車來。

🎁 Dialog 聽力對話

Brenda : Oh, my God. Are you okay?
　　　　噢，我的天啊。你還好嗎？

Rick : Yes, I'm fine. Are you hurt?
　　　　還好，我沒事。你有受傷嗎？

Brenda : No, no I'm fine. Oh no! Look at my car!
沒有，我沒事。噢，不！你看我的車！

Rick : I am sorry. I didn't see you. I was talking on my cell phone.
我很抱歉。我沒有看到你，我當時正在講手機。

Brenda : Hey, you were at the party.
嘿，你剛才也有參加派對。

Rick : Right. My name is Rick.
沒錯。我叫瑞克。

Brenda : I'm Brenda.
我是布蘭達。

Rick : I am really sorry about this, Brenda. Do you have **insurance**?
我真的很抱歉，布蘭達。你有保險嗎？

Brenda : Yes I do. Do you have **insurance**? You were the one who hit me.
是的，我有。那你有保險嗎？是你撞到我的。

Rick : Tell you what. It's late right now. Let me give you my card. I will take down your number and we can talk about this tomorrow.
不然這樣吧，現在很晚了，我給你我的名片。我會記下你的電話號碼，我們明天再討論這件事。

Brenda : Sure. Just let me write down your license plate number. It seems like all kinds of people are crashing into me today.
好。我先記下你的車號。看來，今天大家都衝著我來。

Rick : Yah, I saw the scene with Paul earlier.
沒錯，我看到之前保羅那一幕了。

Brenda : You did? How embarrassing.
你看到了？真丟臉。

Rick : Nah, I thought you handled yourself well.
不，我認為你應對得很好。

Brenda : Well, it isn't every day a small town actress spills a drink on someone like that. I doubt I will ever forget it.
嗯，小鎮演員可不是每天都把飲料潑在那種人身上，我想我是難以忘懷了。

Rick : You're an actor?
你是演員？

Brenda : Aren't half the people working in restaurants?
餐廳裡大半的人不都是嗎？

Rick : I suppose so.
我想也是。

Brenda : Here's my number, Rick. Let's talk tomorrow.
這是我的電話，瑞克。我們明天再談。

Keywords 聽力關鍵字

☑ in particular — 特別

☑ take a liking to — 喜歡

☑ recognize — 認識

☑ sharp dresser — 穿衣行家

☑ impolite — 不禮貌的

☑ crash — 碰撞

☑ insurance — 保險

☑ license plate — 汽車牌照

☑ scene — 場景

☑ handle oneself — 控制自己

☑ doubt — 懷疑

MEMO

....

....

....

....

....

....

....

Questions 聽力關鍵題

1. _____

Ⓐ She is a sharp dresser and likes to have a good time.
Ⓑ She is funny and pretty.
Ⓒ She doesn't worry about anything.
Ⓓ She wants to be an actor.

2. _____

Ⓐ Brenda lost her cell phone.
Ⓑ Brenda got another speeding ticket.
Ⓒ Somebody crashed into her car.
Ⓓ Brenda spills another drink in a small town.

Answers and Translations 聽力中譯與解答

1. Why did the customers like Brenda?
   為什麼客人喜歡布蘭達？

   Ⓐ 她會穿衣服且看起來很開心。　Ⓑ 她有趣且漂亮。
   Ⓒ 她什麼事也不擔心。　Ⓓ 她想當個演員。

2. What happened in the parking lot?
   停車場發生了什麼事？

   Ⓐ 布蘭達掉了她的手機。　Ⓑ 布蘭達又被開了一張罰單。
   Ⓒ 有人撞到她的車。　Ⓓ 布蘭達在小鎮又翻倒一杯飲料。

答案：1→B　2→C

Chapter 4

Brenda in the Big City (Part II)
布蘭達在大城市（二）

In this chapter, the training is going to be difficult. Listen to the CD first. After finishing an article, if you still don't understand what it's all about, take a quick look at the article, and then repeat listening to the CD until you fully understand it.

這一章的訓練要困難一些。直接聽 CD 的內容，聽了一遍後，若你還是不懂內容在說什麼，快速翻一遍課文，再重複聽 CD，直到你完整了解內容。

Getting into the Swing of Things

漸入佳境

Track-32

Start from here

It wasn't long before Brenda got the hang of her serving job. She had enough hours at work to pay her bills and enough tips to pay off her old debts. Brenda started to feel more comfortable in the big city. By this time, she had started to make some new friends. Andrew, a co-worker from the restaurant, was interested in acting too. Brenda and Andrew would often go to shows or plays together and then talk about them over coffee. Brenda and Andrew had no intention of dating each other. They were just friends. Besides that, Andrew was gay. Andrew often encouraged Brenda to get into the dating scene. Brenda said she wasn't interested in meeting boys in smoky clubs or bars. She felt that if it was the right time for her to meet someone special, then that special guy would appear.

中譯

很快地，布蘭達對女侍的工作越來越駕輕就熟。她的底薪與小費，都足以幫她付清帳單費用。布蘭達開始對居住在大城市，感到自在。同時，她也開始交新朋友：安德魯是餐館的同事，他也對表演工作有興趣。布蘭達和安德魯常會一起去看表演或戲劇，然後邊喝咖啡邊討論。不過，兩個人對約會交往倒是一點兒興趣也沒有；大家單純只是朋友而已。再說，安德魯是同性戀，他常鼓勵布蘭達去約會，但布蘭達並不想在充滿煙味的俱樂部或酒吧裡找對象。她覺得一旦時機到了，真命天子自然會出現。

📦 Dialog 聽力對話

Andrew : Honey, when are you going to get out and find yourself a man?

親愛的，你什麼時候才會出去為自己找個對象？

Brenda : Why do you care so much if I have a boyfriend or not?

你幹嘛這麼在乎我有沒有男朋友？

Andrew : I'm just looking out for you. You've been in town for more than eight months, and you haven't gone on one date.

我只是為你著想嘛。你到城裡已經八個月了，卻還沒約會過半次。

Brenda : I haven't seen anyone I liked yet.
我還沒遇到喜歡的人。

Andrew : Are you sure you don't have some small-town sweetheart waiting for you back home?
真的不是因為故鄉有癡情郎在等你？

Brenda : Yeah, I'm sure about that. I just have other priorities.
真的沒有。只是我現在有更重要的事。

Andrew : Like what?
像是什麼？

Brenda : I want to get my career going. I don't want to spend all my time chasing boys.
我希望先拼事業，而不是花時間去追男生。

Andrew : You want to become famous and then all the boys can chase you!
你想成名，然後讓所有男人來追你！

Brenda : Yeah, that's more like it.
嗯，差不多吧。

Andrew : That isn't a bad plan.
這計畫不賴。

Keywords 聽力關鍵字

☑	get the hang of something	更上手
☑	debt	債務
☑	intention	意欲
☑	date	約會
☑	gay	同性戀
☑	encourage	鼓勵
☑	smoky	充滿煙味的
☑	priority	要事
☑	chase	追逐
☑	career	事業

MEMO

....
....
....
....
....
....
....
....
....

Questions 聽力關鍵題

1. _____

Ⓐ They watched movies and went to smoky bars.
Ⓑ They paid off her debt and drank coffee together.
Ⓒ They chased boys together.
Ⓓ They went to shows and plays together.

2. _____

Ⓐ She has other priorities.
Ⓑ She has a small-town sweetheart waiting for her.
Ⓒ Her restaurant job is more important than boys.
Ⓓ She's a bad planner and doesn't know what she wants.

Answers and Translations 聽力中譯與解答

1. What did Andrew and Brenda do together?
安德魯和布蘭達都一起做些什麼？

Ⓐ 他們一起看電影，去充滿煙味的酒吧。　Ⓑ 他們把債務都還清了，然後一起喝咖啡。

Ⓒ 他們一起追男生。　Ⓓ 他們一起去看表演、戲劇。

2. Why doesn't Brenda have a boyfriend?
為什麼布蘭達沒有男朋友？

Ⓐ 她有其他的重要事。　Ⓑ 她在家鄉有個青梅竹馬在等她。

Ⓒ 她餐廳的工作比男人更重要。　Ⓓ 她拙於計畫未來，不知道自己想要什麼。

答案：1→D　2→A

176

Unit 2

Getting Some Class

上課充實自己

Track-33

Start from here

Brenda continued to look for acting work, but was unsuccessful. Andrew suggested she try some acting classes. Classes were an excellent way to make contacts. Brenda agreed. Making some friends in the acting business was exactly what she needed. Plus, she felt she could be getting a bit rusty since she had been away from school for so long. Brenda did some research on the Internet about good acting schools and classes downtown. There were a lot of different schools offering a range of techniques and styles. She wasn't sure how to choose a well-known school that was also affordable, so Andrew gave her a list of schools and classes that he had heard good things about. Armed with that list Brenda walked the downtown streets looking for a place that was right for her. When she saw the Big City School of Performing Arts, she knew she had found the right place.

The school building was old and traditional. She could see dancers on their way to class with ballet shoes in hand. There were also musicians with their trumpets, saxophones and guitars. She even witnessed some students rehearsing their lines on the lawn. Brenda felt excited. She wanted to be a part of this environment. She felt the creativity in the air. She entered the building and found the information desk.

中譯

　　布蘭達持續找尋表演工作，但不是很成功。安德魯建議她去上點表演課，因為上課是建立門路的好方式。布蘭達同意了；透過表演課來結交一些朋友，正是布蘭達需要的。再者，她覺得自己離開學校已有一段時日，技巧上也有些生疏。布蘭達在網路上做了一些搜尋，找尋市中心優秀的表演學校和課程。提供不同的技巧、風格的學校很多，她不知道要怎樣選一家知名，自己又付得起學費的學校，所以安德魯給了她一個名單，上面有一些他聽過還不錯的學校和課程。有了這個名單，布蘭達到了市中心，找尋適合自己的地點。當她看到「大城市表演藝術學校」時，她知道自己找到了適合的地方。

　　學校的建築是舊式且傳統的。她看到很多手上拎著舞鞋，準備去上課的舞者。還有一些帶著喇叭、薩克斯風和吉他的音樂家。她還看到一些學生，在草地上練台詞。布蘭達覺得很興奮，她很想成為這裡的一員。她能感受到空氣中散發的創意。於是她進了大樓，找到了服務台。

Dialog 聽力對話

Brenda : Hi. I want to get some information about acting classes here.

嗨，我想要索取一些關於表演課程的資料。

Reception : OK. No problem. There are some booklets over there describing our classes. Will this be your first acting class?

好的，沒問題。那裡有一些介紹課程的手冊。這是你第一次上表演課嗎？

Brenda : No, I studied acting in university, but it seems film companies don't recognize my school as being very valuable.

不，我在大學修過表演課，但電影公司似乎覺得我的學校不夠大。

Reception : I see. Well, I can assure you this is a reputable school. We've had many stars get their start here.

我了解，我可以向你保證這所學校的聲望。有很多明星都是從這裡起家的。

Brenda : Really? Like who?

真的嗎？例如誰？

Reception : Come this way. I'll show you our wall of fame.

請跟我來，看看我們的星光之牆。

Brenda	:	Cool. 太棒了。

Reception : Max Dellington, Brad Schmidt, Julian Soar and David Duke.

馬克斯・達林頓、布萊德・史密特、朱立・安索爾和大衛・杜克。

Brenda : They all went to school here?

他們都上這個學校嗎？

Reception : They sure did.

沒錯。

Brenda : Do you have classes in the morning?

今天早上這裡有課嗎？

Reception : Sure do. We have a new class called "TV and Commercials". Do you have any TV experience?

當然，我們有一個新課程，叫做「電視與廣告」。你有任何電視相關經驗嗎？

Brenda : None, actually.

事實上，沒有。

Reception : Then, I think you might find that class very valuable. We have an extraordinary director from LA called Raymond Beavis teaching that class.

這樣，你應該會覺得那堂課獲益良多。我們有個很棒的洛杉磯導演，雷蒙・畢為斯，來主導那堂課。

Brenda : When does the class start?
課程什麼時候開始？

Reception : Next Monday. There are only a few spaces left so you should decide quickly.
下週一。名額所剩不多，所以要報名就要快。

Brenda : I've decided already. I want to sign up.
我已經決定了，我要報名。

Reception : We take Visa, Mastercard and cash.
我們接受 Visa、萬事達卡和現金。

Brenda : Cash please.
我付現金。

Keywords 聽力關鍵字

☑ continue   持續

☑ unsuccessful   不成功

☑ contact   聯繫；門路

☑ rusty   生疏

☑ research   搜尋

☑ internet   網際網路

☑ technique   技術

☑ affordable   可負擔的

☑ armed   拿著

☑ trumpet   喇叭

☑ saxophone   薩克斯風

☑ rehearse   排練

☑ lawn   草地

☑ booklet   手冊

☑ valuable   有價值的

☑ assure   保證

☑ reputable   有聲望的

M E M O

Questions 聽力關鍵題

1. _____

Ⓐ She wanted to learn new techniques and make contacts.
Ⓑ She wanted to learn more about wine and fine dining.
Ⓒ She wanted to meet boys.
Ⓓ She wanted to become a musician.

2. _____

Ⓐ Max Dellington, Brad Schmidt, Julian Soar and David Duke.
Ⓑ Other waiters and waitresses.
Ⓒ She would meet Andrew in class.
Ⓓ She would meet new friends, contacts and teachers.

Answers and Translations 聽力中譯與解答

1. **Why did Brenda want to go back to school?**
   為什麼布蘭達想回去上課呢？

   Ⓐ 她想學習新的技巧，建立一些門路。**Ⓑ** 她想要學習更多品酒和美食的知識。

   Ⓒ 她想要認識男人。　　　　　　　**Ⓓ** 她想要成為音樂家。

2. **Who would she meet in her new classes?**
   布蘭達會在新課程碰到哪些人？

   Ⓐ 馬克斯・達林頓、布萊德・史密特、朱立・安索爾和大衛・杜克。**Ⓑ** 其他男侍和女侍。

   Ⓒ 她會在課堂上碰見安德魯。　　　　**Ⓓ** 她會有新朋友、新門路和新老師。

答案：1→Ⓐ　　2→Ⓓ

上課第一天

Start from here

　　It was Monday morning, the first day of Brenda's new class. She found her classroom on the second floor of the school. The room was spacious with hardwood flooring and one wall was fully mirrored. There were no desks to sit in, but some boxes were scattered around the room. Brenda evaluated her new classmates. There was a wide range of people who had signed up for this class. She counted about 15 students in all. Most students were in their twenties like Brenda, but she did notice some older students. One was a man named Richard, tall and handsome, and about forty years old. Another woman looked about the same age. Her name was Rita. The one guy who stood out in the crowd didn't introduce himself. He just sat quietly in the corner. He was wearing worn-out sweat pants and a T-shirt. His hair was long, brown and curly. It looked like a haircut was well overdue. While all the other people in the classroom were busy mingling, he just sat.

At ten o'clock, everyone started to wonder where the teacher could be. They started to whisper about who he was and what he might look like. Everyone was very surprised when the man with long, brown, curly hair stood up and told everyone to sit in a circle.

中譯

　　星期一早上到了，這是布蘭達新課程的第一天。她在學校二樓找到了教室，教室很大，有硬木地板，和一面鏡子牆。教室裡沒有課桌椅，但有一些散放的箱子。布蘭達打量了一下新同學；這堂課有形形色色的人報名。她算了算，總共是十五個學生，大部分的學生都跟布蘭達一樣，二十多歲左右，但她也發現幾個較年長的學員。有一位男士，名叫理查，人很高、很英俊，大約四十歲。另一位女士看起來差不多一樣的年紀，名叫莉塔。人群中有一個特別的男子沒有介紹自己，他只是靜靜地坐在角落。他穿著老舊的運動褲、套頭襯衫，留有棕色、捲捲的長髮，看來他早該去理髮了。當教室裡的其他人忙著彼此認識，他只是坐著不動。

　　到了十點鐘時，大家開始奇怪老師在哪裡。他們開始竊竊私語，到底老師是誰、長得什麼模樣。當那個棕色、長捲髮的男人站起來，叫大家坐成一個圓圈時，大家都很驚訝。

🎁 Dialog 聽力對話

Brenda : Who are you?

你是誰？

Raymond : I am your teacher, Raymond. I will be traveling with you on a journey for the next four months.

我是你的老師，雷蒙。我會在之後的四個月，和大家一起度過。

Brenda : You're our teacher?

你是我們的老師？

Raymond : I will be your instructor, yes. As we **explore** each other and ourselves.

是的，我是你們的指導老師，陪大家一同探索彼此和自己。

Mike : (whispers) Oh man, this guy sounds a bit **fruity**.

（私語）天啊，這個男人聽起來好俗。

Raymond : Now that we are sitting in the circle, it's time for us to **introduce** ourselves. Start with your name, then where you are from and why you are here.

既然現在大家已經坐成一個圓圈，是該介紹自己的時候了。從名字開始，然後再說說你來自哪裡，為什麼會到這裡。

Mike : I'm Mike, I am from this city. I'm in this class because I want to learn more about television and commercials.

我叫麥可，我是本地人。我修這堂課是因為，我想要學習更多和電視、廣告有關的事。

Brenda : I'm Brenda. I just moved here from Clayson. I'm an actor without a lot of film or television experience, so I am hoping I can get the skills I need in this class.

我叫布蘭達，剛剛從克雷森搬過來，我是演員，但沒有很多電視、電影相關經驗，所以我希望能在這堂課學到一些技巧。

Richard : Hi, I'm Richard. I am from Saskville. I am not sure why I am here yet, but I want to learn.

嗨，我是理查，來自薩斯維爾。我不確定自己為什麼會來到這裡，但我想要學東西。

Raymond : All right, everyone, that's great. I want everyone to choose a partner now. It doesn't matter who.

好，大家做得很好。現在我要大家選個搭檔，誰都可以。

Brenda : Will you be my partner?

你可以當我的搭檔嗎？

Eric : Sure.

當然可以。

Raymond : It's time now for **massage**.

按摩的時刻到了。

Brenda	:	What? 什麼？

Raymond	:	We will begin each class with **massage**. Choose who will give and who will **receive**. 我們這堂課先以按摩開場。決定一下，兩個人中，誰是按摩者，誰是被按的那個人。

Brenda	:	Why do we have to do this? 為什麼要做這個？

Raymond	:	Acting is a **process** of giving and receiving. Don't be embarrassed. 表演是一個施與受的過程。不必不好意思。

Brenda	:	Oh man. I'll give first, I guess. 天啊，我想我先當按摩者好了。

Eric	:	Sure. 好。

Brenda	:	This is really **weird**. 這真的好怪。

Keywords 聽力關鍵字

☑ **spacious**	寬敞的
☑ **hardwood**	硬木
☑ **mirror**	裝置鏡子

☑ scatter   散亂

☑ evaluate   評估

☑ sign up for (something)   報名

☑ in all   總和

☑ introduce   介紹

☑ explore   探索

☑ fruity   俗氣

☑ massage   按摩

☑ receive   接受

☑ process   過程

☑ weird   怪異的

MEMO

....

....

....

....

....

....

....

....

....

Questions 聽力關鍵題

1. _____

Ⓐ Everyone was the same age as Brenda.
Ⓑ Everyone was younger than Brenda.
Ⓒ Everyone was much older than Brenda.
Ⓓ There was a range in ages.

2. _____

Ⓐ He wore a suit and tie.
Ⓑ He looked clean and tidy.
Ⓒ He wore old baggy clothes and had messy hair.
Ⓓ He looked professional.

Answers and Translations 聽力中譯與解答

1. How old were the students in Brenda's class?
   布蘭達班上的同學年紀多大？

   Ⓐ 每個人都和布蘭達一樣大。　　Ⓑ 每個人都比她年輕。
   Ⓒ 每個人都比她年長許多。　　　Ⓓ 在一個範圍內。

2. What kind of appearance did the teacher have?
   老師的外表如何？

   Ⓐ 他穿西裝、打領帶。　　　　Ⓑ 他看起來很乾淨、整齊。
   Ⓒ 他穿著一件很舊、很寬鬆的　　Ⓓ 他看起來很專業。
   　　衣服、頭髮很亂。

答案：1→D　2→C

190

Unit 4

Teaming up with Eric

與艾瑞克一組

Start from here

After a few weeks, Brenda felt more comfortable in her acting class. She did find some of her instructor's methods to be a bit strange, but she always left the class feeling inspired. The projects and assignments for the class were always with the other students. This meant that Brenda was rehearsing in her free time a lot, which made her feel great because she had missed performing. This week, she was assigned to work with Eric. They were to create a scene on their own, without a script.

Raymond told the class to find their partner. After the entire class was teamed up, he gave out further instructions.

中譯

　　幾週後，布蘭達在表演課裡，感到比較自在了。她覺得老師的方法都有些奇怪，但她每次下課，都會感到有所啟發。課堂的企畫和作業，都是和其他學生一起做的。也就是說，布蘭達可以利用自己空餘的時間，多加排演，這讓她覺得很好，因為她以前一直很想念表演工作。這週，她被指定到和艾瑞克一組。他們要自己在沒有劇本的情形下，想一個故事情節。

　　雷蒙告訴全班，自己找搭檔。在全班都分好組後，他給大家進一步的指示。

🎁 Dialog 聽力對話

Raymond　：　All right, now that you are in pairs, we're ready to begin.

好了，現在大家都分好組了，就可以開始了。

You will create a drama with the things you already have. You're going to get to know your partner.

你們要利用現有的東西，創造一齣戲，你會更認識你的搭檔。

Eric　　：　Are you ready to get to know me, Brenda?

布蘭達，你準備好要來認識我了嗎？

Brenda　：　I hope so.

應該是吧。

Raymond	:	Now choose which person will be revealing something.

現在選一個先「坦白」的人。

Eric	:	Do you feel like revealing something?

你想要「坦白」一些事嗎？

Brenda	:	Not exactly — how about you?

不是很想，你呢？

Eric	:	I'm an open book.

我為人坦蕩蕩，沒什麼秘密。

Brenda	:	All right. Raymond, Eric will "reveal".

好的，雷蒙，艾瑞克說他願意「坦白」。

Raymond	:	Great. Now, Brenda I want you to take Eric's backpack and go through his things.

太棒了，布蘭達，現在我要你打開艾瑞克的背包，看看每一樣東西。

Eric	:	What?

什麼？

Brenda	:	Oh, I can't go through someone's things.

噢，我不要翻別人的東西。

Raymond : This is the **assignment**. This way, you can choose the things that you think are interesting about Eric and from that we will create a drama.

這是作業，這樣你可以選擇看起來有趣的東西詢問，然後創造一個故事情節。

Brenda : Well, it looks like you are not an open book Eric, but an open **backpack**.

看來不是你坦蕩蕩，而是你的背包要坦白囉。

Eric : Ha ha...

哈哈。

Keywords 聽力關鍵字

☑ comfortable	自在的
☑ method	方法
☑ inspired	受到啟發的
☑ project	計畫
☑ assignment	作業
☑ scene	情景；一幕（戲劇）
☑ script	劇本
☑ team up with	和……一組
☑ reveal	揭露；坦承
☑ backpack	背包

Questions 聽力關鍵題

1. _____

Ⓐ They were difficult and demanding.
Ⓑ They were fun and exciting.
Ⓒ They were strange but inspiring.
Ⓓ They were easy and fun.

2. _____

Ⓐ Dancing and singing.
Ⓑ Going for beer after work with her coworkers.
Ⓒ Reading and watching TV.
Ⓓ Rehearsing with her classmates.

Answers and Translations 聽力中譯與解答

1. What did Brenda think about the teacher's methods and assignments?
布蘭達對老師給的方法和作業，有何看法？

Ⓐ 它們都很難、要求很高。　　Ⓑ 它們都很有趣、很刺激。
Ⓒ 它們都很奇怪，但很有啟發性。　Ⓓ 它們都很簡單、很有趣。

2. How did Brenda spend a lot of her free time?
布蘭達如何打發自己閒暇時間？

Ⓐ 跳舞、唱歌。　　　　　　Ⓑ 工作下班後，和同事一起喝啤酒。
Ⓒ 閱讀、看電視。　　　　　Ⓓ 和同學一起排練。

答案：1→C　2→D

Unit 5

Inside the Backpack

背包的秘密

Start from here

Eric was reluctant to hand over his backpack. Brenda wondered what was inside the pack that was making Eric seem so embarrassed. When she opened the pack, she found normal things a student would have. There were notebooks, textbooks, pencils and paper. She found his lunch too: a sandwich, some cookies and an apple. She found his address book, which looked pretty standard, with phone numbers, addresses and names. At the bottom of his bag, she found some shoes and gym clothes. She thought he must work out after class. Everything seemed pretty normal until she found a tape recorder. It was a small, light-weight recorder, which could be hidden in a pocket if you wanted to spy on people and record them secretly.

中譯

　　艾瑞克不太願意把他的背包交出來，布蘭達好奇裡面有什麼東西，會讓他這麼尷尬。當她打開背包時，她看到一些學生常有的東西，像是筆記本、課本、鉛筆和紙。她也看到了艾瑞克的午餐：一個三明治、幾個餅乾和一個蘋果。她還看到了他的通訊錄：一個很標準的聯絡記事本，裡面有電話號碼、地址和姓名。在背包的最底部，布蘭達看到一雙鞋子和運動服，她猜想艾瑞克在上完課後，一定會去運動。每樣東西看起來都很平常，直到她看到一個錄音機。那是個很小、很輕的錄音機，如果想要偷偷監視某個人，可以把這錄音機放在口袋裡，錄他們的説話內容。

🎁 Dialog 聽力對話

Brenda : Ah ha! What is this?
哈！這是什麼？

Eric : Ah... it's nothing.
啊……沒什麼重要的。

Brenda : Nothing? I will be the judge of that. How do I turn this thing on?
是這樣嗎？我先看看再説。要怎麼開動？

Eric : Oh no.
噢，不。

Brenda : There it is.
有了。

Recorder :You are so beautiful... to... ME!!!!
（歌聲）我 .... 覺得你好漂亮！

Eric : Oh no. Now, you've found me out.
噢，現在你發現我的秘密了。

197

Brenda : You're a singer, Eric?
你是個歌星啊？艾瑞克。

Eric : Well, obviously no, I'm a terrible singer. But I am learning how to sing.
呃，聽也知道不是。我歌唱得很糟，但我正在學。

My singing teacher makes me **record** my classes, so I can hear myself improve.
歌唱老師叫我要在課堂上錄音，聽自己的聲音，才能進步。

Brenda : I think it's great you're taking singing lessons.
我覺得你在上歌唱課，是很棒的一件事。

Eric : (**upbeat**) You think my singing is great?
（很樂）你覺得我唱得很好嗎？

Brenda : Well, no... not yet. But it is great that you're trying to learn.
呃，不，還沒很好啦，但肯去學就很偉大了。

Eric : That's what my **Mom** says too.
我媽也這麼說。

Brenda : I think we can use this **tape recorder** for the project.
我想我們可以用這個錄音機，來做這個作業。

Eric : Do I have to sing?
我得唱歌嗎？

Brenda : Nah, we can skip that if you want. Let's use the tape recorder for some kind of secret agent story.

不了，你不想，我們就略過。我們可以用這個錄音機，發展出一個密探的故事。

Eric : Sure. We can be double agents.

好啊，我們可以當雙面間諜。

Keywords 聽力關鍵字

☑ reluctant	不情願的
☑ normal	平常的
☑ address book	通訊錄
☑ standard	標準
☑ work out	運動；健身
☑ tape recorder	錄音機
☑ lightweight	很輕的
☑ spy	監視
☑ judge	裁判
☑ record	錄音
☑ upbeat	心情很好的
☑ secret agent	密探
☑ skip	略過
☑ double	雙重的

Questions 聽力關鍵題

1. _____

Ⓐ A sandwich, some cookies and an apple.
Ⓑ Pizza and a coke.
Ⓒ Some cookies and a banana.
Ⓓ Some spaghetti.

2. _____

Ⓐ Workout clothes and shoes.
Ⓑ An address book with phone numbers.
Ⓒ A tape recorder.
Ⓓ A picture of his girlfriend.

Answers and Translations 聽力中譯與解答

1. What was Eric's lunch?
艾瑞克的午餐是什麼？

Ⓐ 一個三明治、幾個餅乾和一個蘋果。　**Ⓑ** 披薩和可樂。
Ⓒ 一些餅乾和一條香蕉。　　　　　　　**Ⓓ** 一些通心麵。

2. What was inside Eric's backpack that made him so embarrassed?
艾瑞克背包裡有什麼東西，讓他感到這麼尷尬？

Ⓐ 運動服裝和鞋子。　　　　　　**Ⓑ** 一本有著電話號碼的通訊錄。
Ⓒ 一個錄音機。　　　　　　　　**Ⓓ** 一張他女朋友的照片。

答案：1→A　2→C

Unit 6

Teamwork

團隊合作

 Track-37

Start from here

Brenda and Eric first wrote their ideas out on paper. Then, they rehearsed the scene together. After a week of rehearsing, they were ready to show the class. It was a big hit. Their scene was very funny and everyone laughed at the right places. Both Brenda and Eric felt proud of their accomplishment. Raymond told them that they had good timing and that they worked well together as a team. Brenda knew what Raymond said was true. She felt very comfortable with Eric. She knew he was a nice guy, considerate, kind and funny. After spending so much time with him in the past week, Brenda even felt she had a crush on Eric. She didn't want to say anything to him about her feelings, because she didn't want to feel embarrassed. After class, Eric pulled Brenda aside.

中譯

　　布蘭達和艾瑞克先把他們的想法寫在紙上，然後一起排練情節。在排練一週後，他們準備好了要在全班面前表演。結果他們的表演很受歡迎，情節很好笑，大家都在適當的時候，笑了出來。布蘭達和艾瑞克倆個人都為自己的成就感到驕傲。雷蒙告訴他們說，他們對時間的控制很好，他們的搭檔也很成功。布蘭達知道雷蒙說的是真的。她覺得和艾瑞克搭檔很自在，也知道他人很好、很體貼、仁慈、有趣。在過去一週中，和艾瑞克相處了許多時間，布蘭達甚至覺得自己好像有些喜歡上艾瑞克。她不想告訴他自己的感覺，因為她不想讓自己感到尷尬。下課後，艾瑞克把布蘭達拉到一旁。

🎁 Dialog 聽力對話

Eric　　: Hey, can I talk with you for a minute?
　　　　　嗨，我可以和你說一下話嗎？

Brenda : Sure, you can walk me to my car.
　　　　　當然，你可以陪我走到車子那裡。

Eric　　: What do you think of what Raymond said?
　　　　　你對雷蒙所說的，有什麼看法？

Brenda : That we're a good team? I think he's right.
　　　　　關於我們是好搭檔嗎？我想他說的很對。

Eric　　: I think he's right too.
　　　　　我也這麼想。

Brenda : Why do you ask?

為什麼這樣問？

Eric : Well, I was just thinking, now that our project is over, I won't see you as much.

我只是在想，這個作業結束了，我可能就不會這麼常看到你。

Brenda : No, I guess not. We'll have new partners next time.

我想不會了，下一次我們會各自有新的搭檔。

Eric : But I liked spending time with you, so I was wondering if you wanted to spend some time with me.

但我喜歡和你在一起的感覺，所以我想知道，你會不會想要花一些時間，和我在一起。

Brenda : Spend some time doing what?

在一起做什麼呢？

Eric : Well, I thought maybe we could start with dinner and a movie.

我在想，也許我們可以從晚餐和電影開始。

Brenda : You mean on a date?

你是說約會嗎？

Eric : Well, yeah... if you want... I mean if you're not interested then...

是的，如果你願意的話，我是說如果你不願意的話……

203

Brenda : No! I'd love to. Let's go out tonight. I have tonight off.

不，我很願意的，今晚好嗎？我今晚休假。

Eric : Great! How about seven o'clock?

好極了，七點鐘怎麼樣？

Brenda : Seven is good.

七點很好。

Eric : I'll pick you up. See you tonight.

我會去接你，今晚見了。

Brenda : OK. See you.

好的，晚上見。

Keywords 聽力關鍵字

☑ write something out	將……寫了下來
☑ a big hit	很成功
☑ accomplishment	成就
☑ timing	時間控制
☑ considerate	體貼
☑ kind	仁慈
☑ have a crush on someone	喜歡上……

Questions 聽力關鍵題

1. _____

Ⓐ They rehearsed the scene together.
Ⓑ They showed the class.
Ⓒ They hit each other.
Ⓓ They wrote their ideas out on paper.

2. _____

Ⓐ They laughed at the right places.
Ⓑ Eric was a nice guy.
Ⓒ They had good timing and were a good team.
Ⓓ They should feel proud.

Answers and Translations 聽力中譯與解答

1. What did Brenda and Eric do first?
布蘭達和艾瑞克一開始做了些什麼？

Ⓐ 他們一起排練情節。　　Ⓑ 他們表演給全班看。
Ⓒ 他們打了對方。　　　　Ⓓ 他們將這個想法寫在紙上。

2. What were Raymond's comments about Brenda and Eric?
雷蒙對布蘭達和艾瑞克有何評語？

Ⓐ 他們都在適當的地方笑了出來。　Ⓑ 艾瑞克是個好人。
Ⓒ 他們時間控制地很好、配合得很好。Ⓓ 他們應該感到驕傲。

答案：1→D　2→C

Unit
7

Shopping on Queen Street

皇后街購物趣

 Track-38

Start from here

Brenda felt like everything was coming together. She had a good job, a fun acting class and now a date with the boy she liked! She felt thankful that she had all day to go shopping for the perfect outfit. She wanted to look sexy and fashionable. Eric always saw her in jeans and T-shirts but tonight was their first date. She wanted to look special.

Brenda decided to shop on a very hip street called Queen Street. She wanted to find an outfit that was original. Queen Street was known for having it all. It had original clothing, knock-off clothing and second-hand clothing. Brenda knew she would find something that suited her style. She didn't want to wear a dress or a skirt because she never wore such girly clothes. Brenda found some cool pants that fit her perfectly. She bought a simple white shirt to go with the pants. She was looking for the final touch. Something that would make Brenda

look sexy and cool; the look only leather can give. She
went into a second-hand shop looking for an old leather
jacket.

中譯

　　布蘭達覺得事情發展越來越好，她有份好工作、有趣的表
演課，又將和一位自己喜歡的人約會。對於可以有一整天的
時間，去逛街、買約會要穿的衣服，她感到非常感恩。她希
望看起來很性感、時髦。艾瑞克總是看到她穿牛仔褲和套頭
襯衫的模樣，但今晚是他們第一次約會。她希望看起來很特
別。

　　布蘭達決定要去一條很時髦的街購物，街名叫做皇后街。
她想要找一件有獨創性的服飾。皇后街以有各式各樣的服裝
聞名，這條街有獨創性的服飾、名牌訪製品和二手服飾。布
蘭達知道她會找到適合自己的衣服。她不想要穿洋裝或裙子，
因為她從不穿這麼女性的服飾。布蘭達找到一些很棒的長褲，
很適合她。她又買了一件簡單的白色襯衫，來搭配那件長褲，
但好像還需要最後一件，少了一件可以讓布蘭達看起來性感、
時髦的東西，這只有皮件做得到。所以布蘭達造訪一家二手
店，找尋一件舊的皮夾克。

🎁 Dialog 聽力對話

Brenda ： Hi, do you have any leather jackets?
　　　　　嗨！店裡有任何皮夾克嗎？

Clerk	:	Yes, we have lots actually. Pick your color.

有，實際上我們有很多件，你可以選自己喜歡的顏色。

Brenda	:	Wow! There are so many. How much are they?

太棒了！好多件呢。價格多少？

Clerk	:	Well, the prices range from 40 to 200 dollars. There are some even cheaper ones for about twenty, but between you and me, they **stink** really bad.

價格從四十元到二百元不等，有些甚至便宜到二十元而已，但別說出去：他們聞起來很糟。

Brenda	:	Good tip. I like this red one. Can I try it on?

說的好。我喜歡紅色這件，可不可以試穿？

Clerk	:	Of course. The mirror is right over here.

當然可以，鏡子在那邊。

Brenda	:	Hmm. Not bad, but this belt looks really **nerdy**.

很不錯，但皮帶不好看。

Clerk	:	Well, all these jackets are from the seventies. That jacket is supposed to look like that.

這些夾克都是七〇年代的，所以看起來就是應該那樣。

Brenda	:	How about I try on this black one?

我可以試試這件黑色的嗎？

Clerk : It may be a bit small.
也許有點小。

Brenda : Oh, it is way too small. I can't even move my arms.
啊，太小了，手臂都不能動了。

Clerk : How about this orange one?
那這件橘色怎麼樣？

Brenda : Orange? I don't know. It's kind of **wild**.
橘色？我不確定，看起來很狂野。

Clerk : What about this brown-orange jacket. I think the color is very **unique**.
那這件棕橘色如何？我覺得這顏色很獨特。

Brenda : Woo! I like that one. Let me put it on. Wow. I love it. How much is it?
喔！那件好，我穿穿看。哇！我好喜歡這件，多少錢？

Clerk : It's one hundred dollars.
一百元。

Brenda : Hmm, I can't really **afford** it. Is there any **discount**?
嗯，有點超出我的預算。可以打折嗎？

Clerk	:	I can only go down to ninety.
		我只能便宜到九十元。

Brenda	:	OK. I'll take it!
		好吧，那我就買了。

Keywords 聽力關鍵字

☑ outfit	服飾
☑ hip	時髦
☑ original	獨特的
☑ knock-off	名牌仿製品
☑ second-hand	二手的
☑ to suit	搭配
☑ girly	女性化的
☑ the final touch	最後修飾
☑ leather	皮件
☑ stink	發臭
☑ nerdy	退流行的；落伍的
☑ wild	狂野的
☑ unique	獨特的
☑ afford	負擔得起
☑ discount	折扣

Questions 聽力關鍵題

1. _____

Ⓐ Girly and cute.
Ⓑ Sexy and cool.
Ⓒ Calm and cool.
Ⓓ Thin and tall.

2. _____

Ⓐ New shoes and a leather coat.
Ⓑ Cool pants, a white shirt and a leather coat.
Ⓒ A dress and a leather coat.
Ⓓ A brown-orange skirt and a leather coat.

Answers and Translations 聽力中譯與解答

1. How did Brenda want to look for her date?
布蘭達希望約會時看起來如何？

Ⓐ 女性化、很可愛的模樣。　　Ⓑ 性感、時髦。
Ⓒ 冷靜、沈著。　　Ⓓ 瘦瘦高高的。

2. What did Brenda buy for her date?
為了這次約會，布蘭達買了些什麼？

Ⓐ 新衣服和一件皮外套。　　Ⓑ 漂亮長褲、白襯衫和皮夾克。
Ⓒ 洋裝和皮外套。　　Ⓓ 棕橘色裙子和皮外套。

解答：1→B　　2→B

Start from here

Eric arrived right on time to pick up Brenda. He told Brenda that he was going to take her to someplace really special. He took her to a restaurant called The Cave. It was special for a few reasons. The restaurant was built to look just like a real cave. The walls were not boring white concrete, but made to look like real rock. There were many private booths and tables: each one seemed to be like its own cave. The place seemed like a maze, small hallways with windy turns and dark corners. Brenda thought the place was very cool. She thought it was even cooler when she noticed that the place mat on each table provided a map of the restaurant. Each table had a special name such as "The Rabbit Den" or "Sleeping Bear Cavern." The map revealed where the bar, kitchen and bathrooms were hidden. The hostess seated them near "The Waterfall."

212

中譯

　　艾瑞克準時來接布蘭達，他告訴布蘭達要帶她去一個很特別的地方。他帶她去一家名叫「石窟」的餐廳。這個餐廳很特別，有幾個原因。餐廳的建造方式，看起來就像是一個真的石窟。牆壁不是乏味的白色水泥，而看起來像是真的石塊。餐廳裡有許多私人包廂和餐桌，每一個看起來都像是獨立的石窟。這家餐廳像是一個迷宮，有著小小的走廊、蜿蜒的小道和黑暗的角落。布蘭達覺得這個地方真是酷極了。更酷的是，她注意到每個餐桌的桌布，都有餐廳的地圖。每張餐桌都有特別的名字，像是兔子洞或沈睡的大熊洞。地圖告訴客人酒吧、廚房、洗手間的隱密位置。為他們領位的女主人，將他們帶到「瀑布」旁邊。

Dialog 聽力對話

Brenda : This restaurant is really different. How did you find out about this place?
這家餐廳真的很不同，你怎麼找到這個地方的？

Eric : Well, actually my aunt and uncle run it.
實際上這是我舅舅和舅媽開的。

Brenda : Excellent. Then, you must know what the most delicious food is to eat here.
太棒了，這樣你就一定知道最好吃的食物是什麼。

Eric : Yes, I do. The fondue.
是的，我知道，最好吃的是乳酪火鍋。

213

Brenda : I've never eaten **fondue** before.

我以前從未吃過乳酪火鍋。

Eric : First, we'll start with bread and we'll dip it into a cheese and wine sauce.

我們要先用麵包來沾乳酪和酒。

Brenda : Sounds yummy.

聽起來好好吃。

Eric : Yes, and then they'll bring us a **slab** of hot rock and we can cook our meat on it. You eat meat, right?

是的，然後他們會拿過來一塊熱石塊，我們要自己煮肉，你吃肉吧？

Brenda : Yes, I do.

是的，我吃。

Eric : And then for dessert, strawberries in chocolate **fondue**.

然後甜點是草莓沾融化的巧克力。

Brenda : Mmm, that sounds delicious. How fitting that we will have a real little fire at our table, in this real little **cave**.

聽起來美味極了。在這個石窟、這個餐桌生火，真是再搭配不過的事了。

Eric : Well, I thought I should keep you busy cooking, so you don't notice how boring I am.

我想要讓你忙著煮菜，這樣你就不會注意到我是個多乏味的人了。

Brenda : I doubt I will ever find you boring, Eric.

艾瑞克，我懷疑自己怎麼可能覺得你很乏味。

Keywords 聽力關鍵字

☑	**on time**	準時
☑	**pick up**	接人
☑	**cave**	洞穴
☑	**concrete**	水泥
☑	**private**	私人的
☑	**booth**	包廂
☑	**maze**	迷宮
☑	**windy**	透風的
☑	**place mat**	餐桌布
☑	**hostess**	女主人
☑	**fondue**	乳酪火鍋
☑	**slab**	大石塊

Questions 聽力關鍵題

1. _____

ⓐ The Waterfall.
ⓑ The Cave.
ⓒ The Sleeping Bear Cavern.
ⓓ The Rabbit Den.

2. _____

ⓐ On the wall.
ⓑ On the table.
ⓒ In the bathroom
ⓓ In the kitchen.

Answers and Translations 聽力中譯與解答

1. What was the name of the restaurant Eric took Brenda to?
   艾瑞克帶布蘭達去的餐廳，叫什麼名字？

   ⓐ 瀑布。　　　　　　ⓑ 石窟。
   ⓒ 沈睡大熊窟。　　　ⓓ 兔子洞。

2. Where was the map of the restaurant?
   餐廳的地圖在哪裡？

   ⓐ 在牆上。　　　　　ⓑ 在餐桌上。
   ⓒ 在洗手間裡。　　　ⓓ 在廚房裡。

答案：1→B　2→A

Unit 9

Giant Theatre

大戲院

Start from here

    After one of the most delicious meals Brenda had ever eaten, it was time to go to the movies. They went to the Giant Theatre. Everything about the theatre was big. The drinks, the popcorn, the seats and the screen were all super-sized. Eric and Brenda discussed which movie they wanted to see. There was a good comedy out, but Eric had already seen it. There was a big blockbuster action flick, but Brenda didn't feel the movie was appropriate. They decided on a drama with a young new star called Matty Diamond. The movie was about a young man who was incredibly brilliant but came from a bad neighborhood. He worked at a university as a janitor until the university found out how gifted he was. Then he was introduced to a psychologist who helped him to find his true calling, which was so much more than washing floors and chalkboards.

中譯

　　在結束豐富的晚餐後，布蘭達決定要去看電影。他們去「大戲院」，這家因其內部供應物品之尺寸而得名，從飲料、爆米花、座位到螢幕，都是超大型的。艾瑞克和布蘭達討論他們想要看哪部電影，有一部喜劇片剛上映，但艾瑞克已經看過了。有另一部賣座的功夫片，但布蘭達並不覺得那部電影很適合看。他們決定要看一部劇情片，主角是一位年輕新星，叫做麥特‧戴蒙。劇情是關於一個很聰明的年輕人，在不好的環境下成長。他在一所大學擔任清潔工人，直到學校發現他的天分後，他被介紹給一位心理醫生，這位醫生幫助他找到他真正該做的事，明白自己不只是個清理地板和黑板的人。

 Dialog 聽力對話

Ticket lady : What movie would you like to see?
你們想要看哪部電影？

Eric : Two tickets for *Under it All*, please.
「心靈捕手」兩張。

Ticket lady : Do you want the 9:30 show or the 10:30 show?
九點半那場？還是十點半那場？

Eric : The 9:30 show, please.
九點半。

Ticket lady	:	Do you want popcorn and a drink for an **additional** two dollars? 你要再加兩元，買爆米花和飲料嗎？
Eric	:	No, thanks. 不用了，謝謝。
Ticket lady	:	Your total is $16.50. 總額是十六塊半。
Eric	:	Here's a twenty. 這是二十元。
Ticket lady	:	The show is in Theatre C, this floor. Go through that hall, and it's on your right. 電影在這層樓的 C 廳，穿過大廳，在你的右手邊。
Eric	:	Thanks. 謝謝。
Brenda	:	We have a few minutes to wait before the show starts. Can we play basketball? 電影還有幾分鐘才開始，要不要玩投籃？
Eric	:	I didn't know you played basketball. 我不知道你還打籃球。
Brenda	:	I do. Care for a friendly **match**? 我是啊，要不要玩場友誼賽？

Eric ： OK. But I'm pretty good.
好的，但我很會玩喔。

Brenda ： So am I, don't worry.
我也是，所以別擔心。

Keywords 聽力關鍵字

☑ super-sized	超大的
☑ discuss	討論
☑ comedy	喜劇
☑ blockbuster	賣座片
☑ action flick	動作片
☑ appropriate	適當的
☑ neighborhood	鄰近地區
☑ janitor	清潔工
☑ gifted	有天分的
☑ psychologist	心理醫生
☑ calling	天職
☑ chalkboard	黑板
☑ additional	額外的
☑ match	球賽

Questions 聽力關鍵題

1. _____

Ⓐ The staff all dressed like giants.
Ⓑ Everything was super-sized.
Ⓒ Brenda didn't know.
Ⓓ Because they had lots of big movies.

2. _____

Ⓐ A Drama..
Ⓑ Action.
Ⓒ Love.
Ⓓ A thriller.

Answers and Translations 聽力中譯與解答

1. Why was the theatre called the Giant Theatre?
   為什麼這家電影院叫做「大戲院」？

   Ⓐ 那裡的員工都打扮的像巨人。　Ⓑ 每樣東西都很大。
   Ⓒ 布蘭達不知道。　　　　　　　Ⓓ 因為他們放映許多大型電影。

2. What kind of movie did they go to see?
   他們最後選了什麼樣的電影？

   Ⓐ 劇情片。　　　　　　Ⓑ 動作片。
   Ⓒ 愛情片。　　　　　　Ⓓ 恐怖片。

答案：1→B　2→A

Unit 10

A Stroll in City Park

市立公園漫遊記

Start from here

They both enjoyed the movie and afterwards it was clear that they didn't want the night to end. So they decided to go for a stroll in the City Park. The moon was full and this provided a lot of light although it was late in the evening. Many people were outside, walking their dogs, bicycling and jogging. As Brenda and Eric walked through the park together, they talked and laughed like they were old friends. They talked about anything and everything. She knew that she never needed to keep any secrets from Eric. He was trustworthy and sincere. Brenda was so happy that she felt as though she might float into the sky. While they were chatting, Eric told Brenda about a recent commercial he had worked on.

中譯

　　他們倆都很喜歡那部電影，電影結束後，他們顯然還不想說再見，所以他們決定去市立公園散步。那天晚上是月圓夜，雖然很晚了，天色卻還挺亮的。很多人都還在戶外溜狗、騎腳踏車、慢跑。他們兩人邊散步，邊談話、說笑，彷彿兩個人是老朋友一般。他們幾乎是無話不談。布蘭達知道她有什麼事都可以跟艾瑞克說，他值得信任，又很真誠。布蘭達很高興，快樂地飄飄然。聊天時，艾瑞克跟布蘭達講他最近參與的一部廣告。

 Dialog 聽力對話

Eric : It was embarrassing. I suppose commercials are like that in the beginning.

很丟臉，我想剛開始的廣告應該都是那樣吧。

Brenda : What did you have to do?

他們叫你做什麼？

Eric : It was a car wash commercial. I had to wash my car and then hop up and down like a rabbit.

那是一個洗車廣告。我要邊洗車，然後像兔子一樣跳上、跳下。

Brenda : Like a rabbit? Why?

像兔子一樣？為什麼？

Eric : I don't know. I told you it was stupid. They wanted me to be excited about washing my car. They kept saying, "You should be more excited, more excited!"

我不知道。我說過這很蠢。他們要我表現出興奮洗車的樣子。他們一直說：「再興奮一點、再興奮一點。」

Brenda : Is it on TV?

電視上有播了嗎？

Eric : Yeah, you can see it on Channel Three. It was really **low-budget**.

有，轉到第三台就有了。這算是低成本的廣告片。

Brenda : Was the money worth the embarrassment?

酬勞跟丟臉的代價有打平嗎？

Eric : The money wasn't bad. I guess I just don't like doing commercials.

酬勞還不錯，或許只是我自己不喜歡拍廣告吧。

Brenda : I think I'd like to try out for some commercials.

我倒滿想試試拍廣告的。

Eric : I want to start my own theatre company. That way I would never have to do stuff I didn't like.

我想創立自己的電影公司，這樣我就可以專做自己喜歡做的事。

Brenda : Do you have anyone in the position of female lead?

你找到女主角了嗎？

Eric : Yes. Her name is Brenda — maybe you know her...?

有，她的名字是布蘭達，你可能也認識？

Keywords 聽力關鍵字

☑ stroll   散步

☑ trustworthy   值得信賴

☑ sincere   真誠的

☑ float   飄浮

☑ low-budget   低成本

☑ position   位置

☑ female   女性

☑ lead   主角

MEMO

....

....

....

....

....

Questions 聽力關鍵題

1. _____

Ⓐ There was a light show.
Ⓑ Many people in the park had flashlights.
Ⓒ It was a new moon.
Ⓓ It was a full moon.

2. _____

Ⓐ She felt happy because she liked Eric.
Ⓑ She had a lot of balloons.
Ⓒ She wanted to touch the moon.
Ⓓ Eric told her all his secrets.

Answers and Translations 聽力中譯與解答

1. Why was there a lot of light in the park even though it was nighttime?
   為什麼雖然已經是晚上了，公園裡還是很亮？

   Ⓐ 有場燈光秀。　　　　　Ⓑ 公園裡有許多人帶了手電筒。
   Ⓒ 有新月的亮光。　　　　Ⓓ 有滿月的亮光。

2. Why did Brenda feel she might float into the sky?
   為什麼布蘭達覺得自己飄飄然？

   Ⓐ 她覺得很高興，因為她喜歡艾瑞克。Ⓑ 她有許多氣球。
   Ⓒ 她想要碰觸月亮。　　　　　　　Ⓓ 艾瑞克告訴她所有秘密。

   答案：1→D　2→A

Chapter 5

Brenda in the Big City (Part III)
布蘭達在大城市（三）

Now, we're going to the most difficult part. Concentrate on listening to the CD. Repeat once if you still don't understand it. Keep going to the questions part. After that, you can check the article to see how much you understand.

現在我們進入本書最困難的部分了。專心的聽 CD 內容，假如有不清楚的地方，可以重播一次。專注地聽，並回答問題，之後再檢視你的聽力成果。

Track-42

Start from here

Brenda was feeling at home in the big city now. She loved everything about the city: the people, the food and the nightlife. There was always something to do. She spent a lot of time with Eric, and she was content except for one thing. She still wasn't doing any real acting. Her friend Andrew recommended she get some work as an extra on a movie set. As an extra, she would be a background character. She wouldn't have any lines or major responsibility, but she could watch and learn how a movie was made. Brenda thought it was a good idea. She found an agent and set up a meeting with him. The agent told her to bring in some pictures and an acting resumé. Brenda didn't have professional photos and her acting resumé was very short, but she took what she had and met with the agent.

中譯

　　布蘭達在這個大城市裡的生活就像在自己家一樣。她喜歡這個城市所有的一切，無論是人、食物還是夜生活。在這城裡總可找到事情做。大部分的時間她都跟艾瑞克在一起，且感到心滿意足，但美中不足的是，她到現在還無法找到一份真正演戲的工作。安德魯建議她去找個臨時演員的工作，也就是當當路人甲。這樣一來，她既不用念台詞，也沒重責大任，卻可以學到電影的製作過程。布蘭達覺得這個提議很好。她找了一位經紀人，且跟他約了時間碰面。這個經紀人叫她帶些照片及演員履歷表過來。布蘭達不但沒有演員宣傳照，演員履歷表也很短，所以只好拿手頭上現有的資料去見那位經紀人。

 Dialog 聽力對話

Mark ： Thanks for coming in today, Brenda. My name is Mark.

謝謝你今天過來，我叫馬克。

Brenda ： Nice to meet you Mark. Here are my photos and my resumé.

很高興能認識你。這是我的照片及履歷表。

Mark ： Your photos are terrible. You should get new ones.

你這些照片看起來很糟，應該要重照幾張。

Brenda : Oh, sorry.
噢，對不起。

Mark : Your resumé isn't very good either, but that doesn't matter to me.
你的履歷表也不好，但那對我來說無所謂。

Brenda : It doesn't?
無所謂？

Mark : No. As an **extra**, you just need to do what you're told and don't make me look bad.
沒錯。當臨時演員只要乖乖聽話，不要讓我沒面子就行了。

Brenda : Oh, I can do that.
哦，那我辦得到。

Mark : Fill out this form here. I need your name, age, eye color, hair color, height and weight. Also any special **skills** you might have. Do you have any special **skills**?
填好這份表。我需要你的名字、年紀、眼睛的顏色、髮色、身高、體重以及你的專長。你有任何特殊專長嗎？

Brenda : I can play basketball.
我會打籃球。

Mark : I see, any dancing or singing?
好。會跳舞或唱歌嗎？

Brenda : No.
都不會。

Mark : Any **martial arts** or other sports?
任何武術或是其他的運動？

Brenda : No.
都不會。

Mark : Then just put basketball under "special **skills**"
那就在「特殊專長」裡寫上籃球。

Brenda : Wait. I can ride horses. Is that special?
等等，我還會騎馬，那算專長嗎？

Mark : Yes, I would say that is special. Do you have an
answering machine?
算，我覺得那還算特長。你有電話答錄機嗎？

Brenda : No.
沒有。

Mark : Well, get one. Otherwise how am I supposed to
get a hold of you?
那就去買一台。要不然我怎麼找你？

Brenda : I'll buy one today.
我今天就去買。

Mark : Pay for **extras** is $7.25 an hour. There is no **overtime**. I'll call you if something comes up.

臨時演員的時薪是七塊二十五分。不用加班。有通告時我會打電話給你。

Brenda : Thanks.

謝謝。

Keywords 聽力關鍵字

☑ nightlife 夜生活

☑ content 滿足的

☑ recommend 建議

☑ extra 臨時演員

☑ responsibility 責任

☑ agent 經紀人

☑ set up 安排；訂立

☑ skill 專長

☑ martial arts 武術

☑ get a hold of someone 聯絡

☑ answering machine 答錄機

☑ overtime 加班

Questions 聽力關鍵題

1. _____

Ⓐ He told her to become a character.
Ⓑ He told her to get a life.
Ⓒ He told her to some work as an extra.
Ⓓ He told her to do some extra work at the restaurant.

2. _____

Ⓐ Her photos and acting Resumé.
Ⓑ A note from her mother.
Ⓒ Someone professional.
Ⓓ A friend.

Answers and Translations 聽力中譯與解答

1. What did Brenda's friend Andrew recommend her to do?
布蘭達的朋友安德魯建議她做什麼？

Ⓐ 叫她成為一位演員。　　Ⓑ 叫她找事情做。
Ⓒ 叫她去當臨時演員。　　Ⓓ 叫她到餐廳做事。

2. What did Mark tell Brenda to bring to the meeting?
馬克要布蘭達面試時帶什麼東西？

Ⓐ 她的照片及演員履歷表。　　Ⓑ 她母親寫的紙條。
Ⓒ 一位懂得演戲的人。　　Ⓓ 一位朋友。

答案：1→C　2→A

An Unexpected Call
意外的來電

Start from here

Brenda was feeling a bit sensitive after such a hurried meeting with Mark. She was certain that he would never call her. But just a week after Brenda met with him, there was a message waiting for her on the answering machine. It was Mark! He had a potential job for her. The message asked if Brenda had appropriate clothing for a rave party. Brenda had never even been to a rave before. She didn't even know what "rave party clothes" were. She decided it didn't matter; she would buy the clothes if she had to. She found Mark's number and called him back.

中譯

　　在匆促的跟馬克見面後，布蘭達感到有點難過，因為她很確信他不會打電話給她。然而就在和馬克見面的一個星期後，她發現話答錄機上有個留言。原來是馬克的留言。他說有份相當具有潛力的工作要給她。留言上問布蘭達有沒有適合在銳舞派對上穿的衣服。布蘭達從未參加過銳舞派對，甚至不知道銳舞派對所穿的衣服是什麼樣子。她心想沒有關係，有必要的話再買。她找到馬克的電話然後打了電話給他。

🎁 Dialog 聽力對話

Brenda : Hello Mark? This is Brenda.
馬克嗎？我是布蘭達。

Mark : Brenda, great. Thanks for calling me back so soon.
布蘭達，太好了。謝謝你這麼快就回電給我。

Brenda : No problem.
沒問題。

Mark : Are you free on Tuesday?
你星期二有空嗎？

Brenda : Yes.
有。

Mark : Great. I have your first job. You'll be a dancer at a **rave party**.
那真是太好了。我幫你找到第一份工作了。你將飾演一位在銳舞派對上的舞者。

Brenda : I told you I wasn't a dancer!
我跟你說過我不會跳舞！

Mark : Don't worry. This is a club scene. You'll be dancing with many other people.
別擔心。這只是一場在俱樂部的場景。還有其他的舞者跟你一起跳。

Brenda : Oh, I can do that.
哦，那我可以演。

Mark : The start time is nine in the morning. Please be early.
開工時間是早上九點，但請提早到。

The address is 96 Wall Eye Lane. Please make sure you have three outfits for them to choose from.
地址是渥艾巷九十六號。請記得帶三套衣服來，以便我們挑選。

Brenda : I need three outfits?
我需要帶三套衣服？

Mark : Yes. Is that a problem?
是的，有問題嗎？

Brenda : No, no problem at all. I can do that.
不，一點也不，這我辦得到。

Mark : When you fill out your form, make sure you tell them you are with this **agency**.
填表時，記得跟他們說你是這家經紀公司派來的。

Brenda : Of course.
那當然。

Mark : Any questions?
還有問題嗎？

Brenda : I just show up there?
我只要到那裡就可以嗎？

Mark : Right. They will do your hair and makeup. Just do as you're told and you'll be fine.
沒錯。到時他們會幫你弄頭髮、化妝。只要照著話做就沒問題。

Brenda : Okay. Great.
好，太棒了。

Keywords 聽力關鍵字

☑ **sensitive** 感傷的；敏感的

☑ **hurried** 匆促的

☑ **potential** 有潛力的

☑ **rave party** 銳舞派對

☑ **agency** 經紀公司

☑ **show up** 出現

Questions 聽力關鍵題

1. _____

Ⓐ She ate something at the meeting that made her feel ill.

Ⓑ She thought the meeting was hurried and he didn't really like her.

Ⓒ She watched a sad movie and wanted to cry.

Ⓓ Because he told her to get out of his office.

2. _____

Ⓐ She won't do the job.

Ⓑ She will buy some clothes.

Ⓒ She will make some clothes.

Ⓓ She won't take any.

Answers and Translations 聽力中譯與解答

1. Why was Brenda feeling a bit upset after her first meeting with Mark?
   布蘭達為什麼在跟馬克面試後感到有些難過？

   Ⓐ 在面試當中她吃了不新鮮的食物，而讓她感到不舒服。

   Ⓑ 她覺得面試太過匆促，馬克應該不喜歡她。

   Ⓒ 她看了一部悲劇電影而想哭。　Ⓓ 因為她被趕出他的辦公室。

2. What will Brenda do if she can't find the clothing she needs for the job?
   布蘭達如果找不到適合的衣服，她會怎麼做？

   Ⓐ 拒演。　　　　　　　　Ⓑ 買一些衣服。

   Ⓒ 做一些衣服。　　　　　Ⓓ 一件衣服都不帶。

   答案：1→B　2→B

Start from here

Now, Brenda was ecstatic. Finally, she was going to be on a real movie set. She didn't care that her part wasn't very important. This was her first real film job. Tuesday was only three days away. That didn't give her much time to find the clothes the movie wanted. What could she do? She couldn't possibly afford to buy three new outfits for dancing in clubs, especially since she would never wear them again. She decided to call on some friends for help. Andrew said that those kinds of clothes weren't his style. Eric said he had some clothes that she could borrow. He had some baggy pants and a few t-shirts. Her classmate Monica said she had some things that would fit Brenda but no shoes. Brenda decided borrowing the clothes was a good idea, but to dance in shoes that didn't fit well was a bad one. She decided to look for some shoes she could take with her.

中譯

　　布蘭達高興的不得了，因為她終於要上電影螢幕了，而她一點都不在乎她的角色。這將是她真正的第一份電影工作。離星期二只有兩天的時間，沒有太多的時間去找戲服了，怎麼辦呢？她沒有錢可以買三套跳舞要穿的衣服，尤其是戲拍完後，根本就不會再穿。她決定打電話向朋友求救。安德魯說那型的服裝不是他的品味。艾瑞克說他有一些寬鬆的褲子及T恤可以借她。她的同學莫妮卡說有合布蘭達尺寸的衣服，但鞋子就不行了。布蘭達想，跟朋友借衣服還行得通，但若借一雙尺寸不合的鞋來穿，就不行了，所以她決定去買雙鞋。

Dialog 聽力對話

Brenda : Thanks for coming with me, Eric. I wouldn't even know where to start to look.

艾瑞克，謝謝你陪我來，不然我真不知道要從何找起。

Eric : No problem. If you have any style questions, you can always come to me.

沒問題。對於造型方面的問題，隨時可以來找我。

Brenda : What about these shoes?

你覺得這雙鞋怎麼樣？

Eric : Well, you may spend all day dancing in them. Do you think they look very comfortable?

你可能要穿著這個跳一整天的舞。你覺得他們看起來很舒服嗎？

Brenda : No, they don't look comfortable at all.
不，看起來一點都不舒服。

Eric : You want a pair of sneakers, like these ones.
你需要的是球鞋，像這雙。

Brenda : Are these the kind of shoes people wear to clubs?
去舞廳跳舞可以穿球鞋？

Eric : Sure, why not?
當然，為什麼不行？

Brenda : Okay. What color do you think?
好，那要什麼顏色呢？

Eric : I think these red ones are the coolest, but you could go for blue if you prefer.
我覺得紅色的最棒，但如果你喜歡藍色的，就買藍色的。

Brenda : No, I like the red ones too. Can you ask the salesperson for a size nine?
不，我也喜歡紅色這雙。你可以請門市人員給我九號鞋嗎？

Eric : No problem. Size nine, red sneakers coming up.
沒問題。九號、紅色球鞋馬上來。

Keywords 聽力關鍵字

☑	ecstatic	極樂的
☑	movie set	電影片場
☑	borrow	借入
☑	baggy	寬鬆的
☑	sneakers	球鞋
☑	salesperson	售貨員
☑	prefer	偏愛

MEMO

Questions 聽力關鍵題

1. _____

Ⓐ He said he didn't trust her.
Ⓑ He was going to wear them to the rave party.
Ⓒ He said those kind of clothes weren't his style, so he didn't have any.
Ⓓ He said they wouldn't fit her.

2. _____

Ⓐ In case she has to run away.
Ⓑ Because she didn't want to hurt her feet while dancing.
Ⓒ Uncomfortable shoes weren't her style.
Ⓓ She wanted to spend a lot of money.

Answers and Translations 聽力中譯與解答

1. Why didn't Andrew give Brenda rave party clothes?
   安德魯為什麼不借給布蘭達銳舞派對的衣服？

   Ⓐ 他說他不信任她。　　Ⓑ 他要穿那些衣服去參加銳舞派對。
   Ⓒ 因為那種衣服不是他的風格，Ⓓ 他說那些衣服的尺寸不合她。
   所以他沒有。

2. Why did Brenda want to buy comfortable shoes?
   布蘭達為何要買穿起來舒服的鞋？

   Ⓐ 以防演戲時需要跑。　　Ⓑ 因為她不想因為跳舞而使她的雙腳
   受傷。
   Ⓒ 不舒服的鞋不是她的風格。　Ⓓ 她想花很多的錢。

   答案：1→C　2→A

243

Start from here

Early Tuesday morning, Brenda packed up her things for her first day on set. In a bag she had three changes of clothes, two pairs of shoes, a magazine and her journal. She was ready, but she felt very nervous. She didn't know anybody at this place, and nor did she know what to do when she got there. She drove to the address. Luckily when she arrived on set, she saw a big sign that pointed where to go. First, the people in costumes looked at the clothing she brought. They told her to wear baggy pants and a tank top with the new red shoes. Then she was sent to hair and make-up. The make-up girl used bright colors and sparkles to make Brenda look like a party girl. Then the hair girl gave Brenda two pigtails and barrettes. When Brenda was finished she looked in the mirror. She barely recognized herself, but she thought the costume was great. The only thing left to do was wait. And wait she did. Two hours went by before anyone even talked to Brenda again. Brenda read a magazine and wrote in her journal. Some of the other extras talked to each other or played cards. Brenda got tired of killing time. She decided to make some new friends.

中譯

　　星期二一大早，布蘭達將她第一天演戲要用的東西裝好。袋子裡有三套衣服、兩雙鞋、一本雜誌及她的日記本。在那裡她一個人都不認識，也不知道到那裡之後要做些什麼。她開車到指定的地址。很幸運地，一到那兒就有一個大標示指示她該去的地方。剛開始，負責戲服的人員看了她帶的衣服，然後叫她穿上那件垮褲、緊身上衣及那雙紅鞋。之後，她就被送去弄頭髮及化妝。化妝師用鮮豔亮彩妝，將布蘭達點妝成一個十足的派對女孩，而髮型造型師將她的頭髮梳成兩條辮子並別上髮夾。造型完畢後布蘭達照了鏡子，她簡直認不出自己了，不過整體的感覺很棒。最後一件要做的事就是等著拍戲。她一直等，等了兩個小時，沒人跟她講話，所以她翻了翻雜誌及寫寫日記。其他的臨時演員不是在聊天就是在玩撲克牌。布蘭達不知道如何來消磨時間，所以決定去交新朋友。

MEMO

🎁 Dialog 聽力對話

Brenda : Hi, I'm Brenda. Is there room for one more?
嗨，我是布蘭達。我可以加入嗎？

Brent : Yeah, you can play cards with us. We'll start a new game when John gets back from the bathroom.
可以，你可以跟我們一起玩牌。等約翰上完廁所，我們就玩新的一局。

Brenda : That would be great. I'm really bored.
太好了，我真是無聊死了。

Brent : In a few hours you may wish you were bored.
幾小時後，你就會這麼希望了。

Brenda : What do you mean?
什麼意思？

Brent : Well, from what I heard, we may spend the rest of the day dancing.
據我所聽到的，我們可能要跳一整天的舞。

Brenda : Is that so bad?
那樣不好嗎？

Brent : Have you ever danced for five hours in a row?
你有連續跳過五小時的舞嗎？

Brenda : No, I guess not.
沒有。

Brent : Well, it's tiring. I did one of these club scenes before.
那很累人的。我以前演過一次像這樣的跳舞場景。

Brenda : So I should thank my lucky stars we're just sitting here?
所以現在能坐在這裡，我應該要感恩？

Brent : That's right. Believe me, later you will be tired.
沒錯。相信我的話，待會你就會覺得很累。

Keywords 聽力關鍵字

☑ **magazine**	雜誌
☑ **journal**	日記
☑ **costume**	戲服
☑ **sparkle**	亮粉妝
☑ **pigtail**	辮子
☑ **barrette**	髮夾
☑ **kill time**	消磨時間
☑ **in a row**	連續
☑ **thank one's lucky stars**	感恩

Questions 聽力關鍵題

1. _____

Ⓐ She followed the other extras.
Ⓑ The make-up girl told her where to go.
Ⓒ She saw a big sign that pointed the way.
Ⓓ She waited until someone came looking for her.

2. _____

Ⓐ She was tired of killing the clock.
Ⓑ She was lonely.
Ⓒ She wanted to take their cards.
Ⓓ She was tired of **killing time**.

Answers and Translations 聽力中譯與解答

1. Once Brenda got to the site, how did she know where to go?
   布蘭達到拍片現場時，她怎麼知道要往哪兒走？

   Ⓐ 跟著其他臨時演員。　　　　Ⓑ 化妝師告訴她如何走。
   Ⓒ 她看到一個大標誌指示她如何走。　Ⓓ 在原地等，直到有人來找她。

2. Why did Brenda decide to make some new friends?
   為何布蘭達決定交些新的朋友？

   Ⓐ 她厭倦了把鐘打壞。　　　　Ⓑ 她感到很寂寞。
   Ⓒ 她想把他們的撲克牌拿走。　Ⓓ 她厭倦了消磨時間。

答案：1→C　2→D

Start from here

Brenda ended up dancing for over six hours. She was tired but she had had a great time on set. As she drove home at the end of day she evaluated her experience. There were many things she liked. She liked a lot of the other extras. She had met some new friends. She liked the food, which was free and delicious. She liked watching the film crew set up shots. She also liked watching the actors. There were some things Brenda didn't care for. She found some people's attitudes were very outrageous and demanding. The main actors seemed snobbish. Some crew seemed over-dramatic. She realized now that Paul Jones, the director she spilt wine on months ago was not the only egomaniac in town. She decided that if she was ever going to make it in acting she didn't want to become like them. When Brenda got home that night she called Eric.

中譯

　　布蘭達最後跳了六個小時的舞。雖然很累，但她跳得很高興。跳完一天的舞之後，她在開車回家的途中，對這次演戲的經驗做了個評估。有很多事情她很喜歡，她喜歡其他的臨時演員、新的朋友，喜歡那裡免費又好吃的食物。她喜歡看片場人員搭景拍戲，也喜歡看演員演戲，但有些事卻讓她很不屑。她發現有些人的態度很無禮而且很苛求。那些主要的演員似乎很看不起人，而一些在場的人員也似乎過於戲劇化。她想起在幾個月前，被她灑到酒的導演保羅。她發覺那個導演不是城裡唯一的臭屁鬼。她心想，如果有一天在演藝圈功名成就的話，絕對不想變成那個樣子。布蘭達到家後，馬上打電話給艾瑞克。

 Dialog 聽力對話

Eric　　：How was your big day?
　　　　　你的大日子怎麼樣？

Brenda：I danced for six hours. Thanks for helping me buy **comfy** shoes.
　　　　　我整整跳了六小時的舞。謝謝你幫我買了雙舒服的鞋。

Eric　　：What did you think?
　　　　　你覺得怎麼樣？

Brenda : It was interesting. They start and stop the music, and you have to do the same thing over and over again.

很有意思。他們放音樂、停音樂，然後一直重複同樣的事。

Eric : Did you meet any big stars?

有沒有跟大明星說到話啊？

Brenda : No, I didn't meet anyone famous, but I did dance behind someone famous though.

沒，沒半個，但我有在一個明星後面跳舞喔。

Eric : Who?

是誰？

Brenda : Mason Lee.

李梅森。

Eric : Wow, what did he look like?

哇，他本人看起來怎樣？

Brenda : Actually he looks a lot shorter in real life than he does in the movies.

他本人看起來比電影上的還矮。

Eric : Not a bad first day. Want to go out for a drink to celebrate?

這個第一天算不錯了。要到外面喝一杯，慶祝慶祝嗎？

Brenda : I would rather you came over for one. I'm **exhausted**.

我倒希望你來我這兒喝一杯，我累死了。

Eric : I'll be over in a half hour

那半個小時後見囉。

Brenda : Great.

好極了。

Keywords 聽力關鍵字

☑	send up	送上來
☑	film crew	片場人員
☑	shot	拍片
☑	attitude	態度
☑	outrageous	粗魯的
☑	demanding	苛求的
☑	snobbish	自負的
☑	over-dramatic	太戲劇化的
☑	egomaniac	自負者
☑	comfy	舒服的
☑	exhausted	筋疲力盡的

Questions 聽力關鍵題

1. _____

Ⓐ She enjoyed seeing the outrageous and demanding people.
Ⓑ Spilling wine on Paul Jones.
Ⓒ Her new red shoes.
Ⓓ The other extras and the free food.

2. _____

Ⓐ She didn't want to be a star.
Ⓑ If she became a star she didn't want to have a bad attitude.
Ⓒ She would like to be just like Paul Jones.
Ⓓ She would always have delicious food on set.

Answers and Translations 聽力中譯與解答

1. What were some things Brenda enjoyed about her first day on set?
布蘭達在片場的第一天，最喜歡什麼？

Ⓐ 她喜歡看無禮且苛求的人。　Ⓑ 把酒灑到保羅‧瓊斯身上。
Ⓒ 她的新紅鞋。　Ⓓ 其他的臨時演員及免費的食物。

2. What did Brenda decide about making it as an actor?
如果當上明星的話，布蘭達希望什麼？

Ⓐ 她不想成為明星。　Ⓑ 她希望自己的態度不要變差。
Ⓒ 她想跟保羅‧瓊斯一樣。　Ⓓ 她希望在片場永遠都有可口的東西吃。

答案：1→D　2→B

Start from here

After Brenda's experience on the film set, she decided she missed the theatre. Eric told her about a small theatre in town that was holding auditions for a new play. Brenda prepared some material. She needed to memorize one classical piece, one contemporary piece and one song. Brenda practiced on her own after work every night for a week trying to get ready for her audition. She had never had to audition for anything before. In university, parts were just handed to her. She was a big fish in a small pond back then, but now she was a small fish in a big pond. She would need to prove herself. The day of the audition arrived too soon. But Brenda felt ready. When she went to the theatre for her audition, she saw many other actors waiting for an audition too. She knew the competition would be tough. She waited for about half an hour, then her name was called. She found her place on stage. She looked into the seats for the face of the director but couldn't see anything. The seats were too dark. She performed her two pieces and then the director asked her to sing.

中譯

　　有過片廠拍片的經驗後，布蘭達想重溫舞台劇。艾瑞克告訴她，城裡有個小劇團正在為新劇徵演員。布蘭達得作些功課：她得背一部古典戲劇與現代劇的台詞，外加一首歌曲。為了這個甄選，布蘭達利用下班時間自己練習了一個禮拜。她以前根本不須要參加甄選，在大學裡，演出機會都是垂手可得。當時她是小地方裡的大人物；而現在卻是大地方裡的小人物，所以必須向人證明她有能力演戲。雖然甄選的日子很快就到來，布蘭達卻已有十足準備。當她到劇院參加甄選時，看到在場有很多競爭者，她知道競爭會很激烈。等了約半個小時，終於輪到她了。她上了舞台，找到定點後，她望向觀眾席，想看導演是誰。可是因為太暗，她什麼也看不清。她表演了兩齣劇後，導演要她唱歌。

 Dialog 聽力對話

Brenda : Does the play have a lot of singing in it?
這部戲有很多地方要唱嗎？

Directo : No, this one doesn't, but I want to hear you sing.
沒有，不過我想聽聽你唱歌。

Brenda : I'm not a very good singer, actually.
我不是很會唱歌，說真的。

Director : I'm sure you are just fine. Sing.
我相信你可以的。唱吧。

Brenda : Really, I would rather not. I can't sing.

真的，我寧可不要。我不會唱歌。

Director : Sing anything. Sing "Happy Birthday".

隨便唱。就唱「生日快樂歌」好了。

Brenda : Okay… Happy birthday to you! Happy birthday to you! Happy birthday dear… you! Happy birthday to you!

好吧⋯⋯祝你生日快樂！祝你生日快樂！祝你生日快樂！祝你生日快樂！

Director : Ahh! That was awful. Whoever said you could sing was wrong!

啊！太可怕了。說你會唱歌的人，真是大錯特錯了！

Brenda : I told you I couldn't sing.

我跟你說過我不會唱歌。

Director : Wait a minute. Don't I know you from somewhere?

等等。我好像在哪裡見過你？

Brenda : I doubt that, Sir. I'm from out of town.

應該不會的，先生。我不是本地人。

Director : No, no, I do know you. Wait a minute... you're that stupid girl that spilt wine on me at that party!

不，我認得你。等等⋯⋯你就是那個在派對中，把酒灑在我身上的笨女生嘛！

Brenda : Oh no!

噢，糟了！

Director : A lot of nerve you have coming here auditioning for me! I would never hire you. You will be serving drinks for the rest of your life!

你還敢來這裡參加我的甄選！我絕對不會用你的。你一輩子幫人家端飲料吧！

Brenda : Well, Sir, I would rather spill drinks on a thousand jerks like you than ever act in your play. Good-bye!

喂，先生，我寧可把酒灑在一千個像你一樣的渾蛋身上，也不屑演你的戲。再──見！

Keywords 聽力關鍵字

- ☑ **material** 材料
- ☑ **memorize** 默記
- ☑ **classical** 古典的
- ☑ **piece** 戲劇
- ☑ **contemporary** 當代的
- ☑ **prove** 證明
- ☑ **competition** 競爭
- ☑ **tough** 困難的
- ☑ **nerve** 勇氣
- ☑ **jerk** 渾蛋

1. _____

Ⓐ She had never wanted to act in a play before.
Ⓑ She liked to go fishing in the pond
Ⓒ She was a small fish.
Ⓓ Parts were handed to her in university.

2. _____

Ⓐ The seats where the director was sitting were too dark.
Ⓑ She didn't care.
Ⓒ She didn't have her glasses on.
Ⓓ She had never met him before.

Answers and Translations 聽力中譯與解答

1. Why had Brenda never auditioned for anything before?
為何布蘭達以前從未參加過甄選？

　Ⓐ 她從來沒想過要演舞台劇。　　Ⓑ 她喜歡在池塘裡釣魚。
　Ⓒ 她是個小人物。　　　　　　　Ⓓ 因為在她大學時，角色幾乎唾手可得。

2. Why didn't Brenda know that the director was Paul Jones before she started her audition?
為何布蘭達在甄選前，不知道那部戲的導演是保羅‧瓊斯？

　Ⓐ 導演坐的觀眾席太暗了。　　Ⓑ 她不在乎。
　Ⓒ 她沒戴眼鏡。　　　　　　　Ⓓ 她從來沒見過他。

答案：1→D　2→A

Unit 7

Meeting Rick

重遇瑞克

Start from here

Brenda was feeling really ripped off after her audition. She couldn't believe she had run into Paul Jones again. She left the theatre in a huff and then sat in her car. "What a jerk!" She was too mad to drive. She knew she needed to calm down or she would probably get another speeding ticket. She replayed the audition in her mind. She wondered, "Did I go too far? Should I have said that to him? Will I ever work in this town again?" Brenda felt terrible. She was so totally absorbed in her thoughts that she didn't notice a man coming over to her car and knocking on the window.

中譯

　　甄選後，布蘭達覺得有種被騙的感覺，她真不敢相信會再碰到保羅·瓊斯。她很火大地離開劇場，然後坐進車裡。「真是渾蛋！」她氣的無法開車。她知道自己必須冷靜下來，否則可能會因超速又被開單。她回想一下甄選的經過，心想：「我會不會太過分了？我應該跟他説那些話嗎？我在這裡還有發展機會嗎？」布蘭達感覺很糟，因為想得出神，沒注意有人走向她的車，敲了她的車窗。

🎁 Dialog 聽力對話

Brenda : Ahh! Oh my God, you scared me!

啊！我的天啊，你嚇到我了！

Rick : Hey, Brenda. Sorry to frighten you. It's me, Rick. Remember? I hit your car a few months back.

嘿，很抱歉嚇到你。是我，瑞克，記得嗎？我在幾個月前撞到你的車。

Brenda : Well, aren't I having many blasts from the pasts today?

我今天真的是冤家路窄了？

Rick : I saw your audition.

我看了你的甄選。

Brenda : Oh, great. How embarrassing. I'm not usually so hotheaded. But that guy really rubs me the wrong way.

噢，太棒了。真是丟臉丟大了。我很少那麼激動的，但是那傢伙真的把我給惹毛了。

Rick : Hey, don't worry about that. He rubs everyone the wrong way. I want to talk to you about your audition.

嘿，別擔心那個。他招惹到每個人了。我想跟你談甄選的事。

Brenda : Okay. What about it?

好，怎麼樣？

Rick : I thought it was really great. I think you're a **natural**.
我覺得你表現得很好，是天生的演員。

Brenda : I think you're trying to be nice to me.
我想你是在安慰我吧。

Rick : I also noticed on your resumé that you have experience riding horses.
我還注意到你的履歷上寫到，你有騎馬的經驗。

Brenda : I won Blue Ribbons at the **rodeo** for the past four years.
四年前，我贏過牛仔競技表演的藍帶獎。

Rick : I think you are perfect for a part in our next movie.
我覺得你很適合演我們下部片的一個角色。

Brenda : You must be joking!
你在開玩笑吧！

Rick : Let me give you my card, Brenda. I'm with Silver Screen Casting. I have a good feeling about this.
我把名片給你，我在「銀幕卡司」工作，我覺得我們可以合作。

Brenda : Oh, wow.
喔，哇。

Rick : We're looking for a new face. That's why I've been checking out small theatre auditions for the past few weeks. Believe me, you have a lot of promise.

我們正在找新面孔，這也是為何在過去幾週內，我一直到小劇院的甄選會上找合適的人選。

Brenda : Wow. I would love to work on your movie. But I have one question.

哇，我很樂意演你的電影，但有一個疑問。

Rick : If it's about Paul Jones, don't worry. I never work with him either.

如果是關於保羅・瓊斯的事，那就不用擔心。我是絕對不會跟他合作的。

Brenda : Great.

太好了。

Keywords 聽力關鍵字

☑ ripped off	被騙
☑ in a huff	生氣地
☑ calm down	冷靜下來
☑ replay	回想；倒帶
☑ absorbed in thought	陷入思緒
☑ knock	敲

☑ a blast from the past	往事重現
☑ hotheaded	一時衝動
☑ rub someone the wrong way	激怒人
☑ natural	天生好手
☑ rodeo	牛仔競技比賽
☑ check out	檢查
☑ a lot of promise	大有潛力

MEMO

....
....
....
....
....
....
....
....
....
....
....
....

Questions 聽力關鍵題

1. _____

Ⓐ She ripped her clothes
Ⓑ She was the big bad wolf.
Ⓒ Because she wanted to get another speeding ticket.
Ⓓ She was feeling ripped off because Paul Jones was such a jerk.

2. _____

Ⓐ He wanted to scare her to death.
Ⓑ He wanted to answer Brenda's questions.
Ⓒ He wanted to talk to Brenda about a part in a movie.
Ⓓ He wanted to hit her car again.

Answers and Translations 聽力中譯與解答

1. Why did Brenda leave the theatre in a huff?
為何布蘭達很生氣的離開劇院？

Ⓐ 她把衣服撕破了。　　　　Ⓑ 她是隻壞的大野狼。
Ⓒ 因為她想再被開一張超速罰單。　Ⓓ 因為保羅‧瓊斯是個渾蛋，而她覺得自己被騙了。

2. Why did Rick knock on Brenda's car window?
瑞克為何敲布蘭達的車門？

Ⓐ 他想嚇死她。　　　　　Ⓑ 他想回答布蘭達的問題。
Ⓒ 他想跟她談一部電影中的角色。　Ⓓ 他想再撞她的車一次。

答案：1→D　2→C

Track-49

Start from here

Brenda drove home after her talk with Rick thinking about what a strange day she was having. "The life of an actor sure has its ups and downs," she thought. When she first came to town no one would consider her. But now it looked like she had what they were looking for. Had one year in the big city really made such a difference? When she got home she called Eric and told him what had happened. Brenda had never told Eric the story of the red wine and white pants, otherwise he would have never sent her to that audition. But it was a good thing he had because now Brenda had a chance to be in a movie, and could even be the star!

中譯

　　布蘭達在和瑞克談話後開車回家，心想真是奇怪的一天。她想：「演員的生活真是起伏不定。」剛到這個城市時，根本沒人會想請她演戲，但是現在，她自己正是人家要找的對象。在大城市裡待上一年，真的有那麼大的差別嗎？回到家後，她打電話給艾瑞克，跟他敘述這天的經過。布蘭達沒跟艾瑞克說過紅酒跟白褲子的事，不然他也不會要她去參加那個甄選。不過也幸好這樣，布蘭達才有機會演電影，甚至還可能成為明星！

🎁 Dialog 聽力對話

Eric : Wow, what a day. I am so happy for you.
哇，真是精采的一天，我真替你感到高興。

Brenda : Well, it seems **my world can change on a dime**. One minute everything is terrible, the next minute I am laughing.
看來我的世界說變就變。前一分鐘還很倒楣；現在又可以開懷大笑了。

Eric : Do you think this Rick guy is for real?
你覺得那位瑞克是說真的？

Brenda : Well, I guess we'll just have to **wait and see**. I'm supposed to call him tomorrow.
嗯，我想只能看著辦了。我明天應該打個電話給他。

Eric : I can't believe you **told off** Paul Jones.
我真不敢相信你罵了保羅‧瓊斯一頓。

Brenda : Neither can I. It just **flew out of my mouth**.
我也不敢相信，但就這麼脫口而出。

Eric : Maybe this Rick guy likes your **spunk**.
也許這位瑞克先生欣賞你的勇氣。

Brenda : Maybe.
也許吧。

Eric : Is this Rick guy handsome?

這位瑞克先生帥嗎？

Brenda : Why? Are you worried?

幹嘛問這個？你擔心啊？

Eric : Just asking.

只是問一下而已。

Brenda : Don't worry, honey. You don't have anything to worry about.

親愛的，別擔心，我跟他什麼都沒有。

Keywords 聽力關鍵字

☑ **ups and downs** 起伏

☑ **difference** 不同

☑ **the world can change on a dime** 世事多變

☑ **tell someone off** 數落；責備

☑ **fly out of one's mouth** 脫口而出

☑ **wait and see** 看著辦

☑ **spunk** 精神；勇氣

☑ **handsome** 英俊的

1. _____

Ⓐ Her day.
Ⓑ The car ride home.
Ⓒ The big city.
Ⓓ The life of an actor.

2. _____

Ⓐ Because she could tell off Paul Jones.
Ⓑ She could tell him the story of the red wine on white pants.
Ⓒ She could meet the handsome Rick.
Ⓓ She could get the chance to be in a movie.

Answers and Translations 聽力中譯與解答

1. What did Brenda think had "its ups and downs"?
布蘭達認為什麼「起伏不定」？

Ⓐ 她的那一天。　　　　Ⓑ 路況。
Ⓒ 大城市。　　　　　　Ⓐ 演員的生活。

2. Why was it a good thing Eric told Brenda about the audition?
為什麼艾瑞克要布蘭達去參加甄選是件好事？

Ⓐ 因為她可以罵保羅‧瓊斯一頓。　Ⓑ 她可以把灑酒事件跟他說。
Ⓒ 可以跟帥哥瑞克見面。　　　　　Ⓓ 她可以有機會演電影。

答案：1→Ⓐ　2→Ⓓ

Start from here

Brenda called Rick the next day. Rick told Brenda to meet him in the afternoon at his office. Brenda went to his office that afternoon and was surprised to find so many people there. The people in the office were all going to make the new movie. They wanted to listen to Brenda read the lines in the script. Brenda read the lines by herself for a little while, and then did her best in front of the small crowd. Afterwards she read, Rick asked her to wait in the hall. Waiting in the hall was not easy. Brenda could hear her heart beating in her ears. It sounded so loud, she was sure everyone could hear it. She wanted this part. She hadn't read all the script but she didn't care. It was a movie and she felt perfect for the part. As Brenda was daydreaming about her future fame, Rick called her back into the room.

中譯

　　布蘭達隔天打電話給瑞克，他請她下午到辦公室一趟。布蘭達到了後，很訝異那邊的人很多。這些人全都是新電影的工作人員，他們想聽布蘭達唸台詞。布蘭達唸了幾段台詞，盡力表現出最好的一面給這一小群觀眾。表演完後，瑞克請她到走廊等。等待並不簡單。布蘭達的耳朵都可以聽到自己的心跳聲，心跳聲很大，她覺得大家一定也都聽得見。她很想得到這個角色。她沒唸完整個劇本，但是她不在乎。這是一部電影，而她很喜歡這個角色。當布蘭達作著以後出名的白日夢時，瑞克請她回辦公室。

🎁 Dialog 聽力對話

Rick : Hi, Brenda. I want to let you know that we are very **impressed** with your reading.

嗨，布蘭達。我想告訴你，大家對你的表現都印象深刻。

We think you are perfect for the part.
我們覺得你很適合這個角色。

Brenda : You do?
真的？

Rick : Yes. I want you to take home this **script** and read it through, then let me know what you think.
真的。我要你把這份劇本帶回去看一遍，然後再跟我說你的看法。

Brenda : Sure! .

沒問題！

Rick : Also, I want you to know that we will start filming next month. You'll need to free up your **calendar**. Can you do that?

還有我要跟你說，我們的電影下個月開拍，所以你得把下個月的行程全部空出來，可以嗎？

Brenda : Sure, no problem.

當然，沒問題。

Rick : And one more thing — we can't pay you.

還有一件事，我們無法付你片酬。

Brenda : What?

什麼？

Rick : Just kidding. What I mean to say is we can't pay you much. The **budget** allows for only ten thousand dollars.

開玩笑的。我是說，我們給的片酬不會很多，照預算我們只能給你一萬。

Brenda : Ten thousand dollars!

一萬！

Rick : So think about it, and give me a call tomorrow.

所以你考慮一下，明天再打電話給我。

Brenda : No need, Rick — I'll do it!

不用了，瑞克——我要演這個角色！

Rick : **Welcome aboard**, Brenda.

布蘭達，歡迎加入。

Keywords 聽力關鍵字

☑ script	劇本
☑ crowd	一群人
☑ hall	走廊
☑ beat	心跳
☑ fame	名望
☑ impressed	感到印象深刻
☑ calendar	行事曆
☑ budget	預算
☑ welcome aboard	歡迎加入

MEMO

Questions 聽力關鍵題

1. _____

Ⓐ In her chest.
Ⓑ In the hallway.
Ⓒ In her day dream.
Ⓓ In her ears.

2. _____

Ⓐ It isn't enough.
Ⓑ It doesn't matter.
Ⓒ It is a lot.
Ⓓ There isn't any.

Answers and Translations 聽力中譯與解答

1. Where could Brenda hear her heart?
   布蘭達可從哪裡聽到她的心跳聲？

   Ⓐ 胸部。　　　　　　Ⓑ 在走廊上。
   Ⓒ 在她的白日夢裡。　Ⓓ 她的耳朵。

2. What does Brenda think about the money they offer her?
   布蘭達覺得他們給她的薪水如何？

   Ⓐ 不夠。　　　　　　Ⓑ 無所謂。
   Ⓒ 很多。　　　　　　Ⓓ 不多。

答案：1→D　2→C

The Call Home

捷報

Start from here

After Brenda met the important movie making people, she went home. She was on cloud nine. Her dream had come true. In her heart she knew she was meant to be an actor and now other people knew it too. She thought about the people who didn't have faith in her. The people that said it would never happen. "Ha! That will show them," she thought to herself. Then she thought about the people that always had faith in her. She wanted to call Eric, but he wouldn't be home from work yet. She could phone her friend Andrew but he was out of town. "Who can I call? Mom and Dad!" This was the call she had wanted to make all year. She raced to the phone.

中譯

跟重要的電影製作群見面後，布蘭達就回家了。她欣喜若狂，因為夢想實現了。她一直相信自己是演戲的料，現在大家也認同了。她想到那些不相信她，說她癡心妄想的人。「哈！這下他們跌破眼鏡囉！」然後她想起那些一直對她有信心的人。她想打電話給瑞克，但他應該還在上班不在家。她想到朋友安德魯，但他出城去了。「我還可以打給誰？爸媽！」這是她整年都在期待的捷報電話，她飛快地跑向電話。

Dialog 聽力對話

Dad : Hello?
喂？

Brenda : Dad, put Mom on the phone too!
爸，叫媽一起聽電話！

Dad : Oh, sorry honey, Mom's in town right now.
喔，親愛的，很不巧，你媽到城裡去了。

Brenda : Dad! I got a part in a movie!
爸！我可以演電影了！

Dad : You're kidding! Sweetheart, that's great.
你沒開玩笑！寶貝女兒，真是太好了。

Brenda : Dad, I'm the main character. It's about a girl on a farm that rides horses. It was just made for me.
爸，我是主要角色。電影是關於農場女孩的故事，這女孩會騎馬。簡直是為我量身定做的。

Dad : Well, sweetie, that is great. Looks like all that time you spent on a horse paid off.

嗯，親愛的，真是太好了。看來你花時間騎馬，也算有所回報。

Brenda : Yeah I think so. Oh Dad, I am so excited. We start filming next month.

嗯，沒錯。爸，我好開心喔。我們下個月就要拍片了。

Dad : How did this all happen?

這一切到底是怎麼發生的？

Brenda : Well, it's a long story starting with a jerk wearing white pants and me holding a glass of red wine.

說來話長。這要從一個白褲子的渾蛋，和拿紅酒的我說起。

Dad : What? Slow down. Start at the beginning.

什麼？慢慢來，從頭開始講。

Brenda : Dad, they are going to pay me ten thousand dollars!

爸，他們要付我一萬元片酬！

Dad : **Holy doodles**.

我的天啊。

Brenda : Yeah, I know. Looks like I can afford to come home for Christmas this year!

我知道。看來今年聖誕節，我可以回家過了！

Dad : Or you can afford to fly us all there!
你也可以出機票錢，讓我們到你那兒過！

Keywords 聽力關鍵字

☑ be on cloud nine   欣喜若狂
☑ have faith in   有信心
☑ race   跑
☑ main character   主要角色
☑ holy doodles   我的天啊

MEMO

....
....
....
....
....
....
....
....
....
....
....
....
....

Questions 聽力關鍵題

1. _____

Ⓐ That she was meant to be an actor.
Ⓑ That she had nine clouds.
Ⓒ That she would never be an actor.
Ⓓ That she had faith.

2. _____

Ⓐ She will become rich and famous.
Ⓑ She will marry Eric.
Ⓒ She will live happily ever after.
Ⓓ All of the above.

Answers and Translations 聽力中譯與解答

1. What did Brenda always know in her heart?
   布蘭達打從心裡知道什麼？

   Ⓐ 她是當演員的料。　　　　Ⓑ 她有如九雲罩頂。
   Ⓒ 她永遠當不成演員。　　　Ⓓ 她有信心。

2. What do you think will happen to Brenda now?
   你認為接下來布蘭達會發生什麼事？

   Ⓐ 她會變得很有名而且有錢。　Ⓑ 她會嫁給艾瑞克。
   Ⓒ 從此過著快樂的日子。　　　Ⓓ 以上皆是。

答案：1→A　2→D

國家圖書館出版品預行編目資料

馬上可以聽懂的超強英語聽力課 / 蘇盈盈, 卡拉卡 合著. -- 新北市：哈福企業, 2020.09
面； 公分. -- (英語系列；65)

ISBN 978-986-99161-3-4(平裝附光碟片)

1.英國語言 2.問題集
805.189　　　　　　　109013435

英語系列：65

. . . .

書名 / 可以馬上學會的超強英語聽力課

合著 / 蘇盈盈・卡拉卡

出版單位 / 哈福企業有限公司

責任編輯 / Mary Chang

封面設計 / Lin Lin House

內文排版 / Co Co

出版者 / 哈福企業有限公司

地址 / 新北市板橋區五權街 16 號

封面內文圖 / 取材自 Shutterstock

. . . .

email ／ welike8686@Gmail.com

電話／（02）2808-4587

傳真／（02）2808-6245

出版日期／ 2020 年 9 月

台幣定價／ 330 元

港幣定價／ 110 元

. . . .

總代理／采舍國際有限公司

地址／新北市中和區中山路二段 366 巷 10 號 3 樓

電話／（02）8245-8786

傳真／（02）8245-8718

. . . .

哈福